I0627948

A Baptism for the Dead

Charles R. Bernard

Madness Heart Press
2006 Idlewilde Run Dr.
Austin, Texas 78744

This is a work of fiction. Names, characters, places, and incidents either are the product of the author's imagination or are used fictitiously. Any resemblance to actual persons, living or dead, events, or locales is entirely coincidental.

Copyright © 2020 Charles Bernard
Cover by Brian Shay

All rights reserved. No part of this book may be reproduced or used in any manner without written permission of the copyright owner except for the use of quotations in a book review. For more information, address: john@madnessheart. press

First Edition
www.madnessheart.press

Charles Bernard

For My Mom

Saqqara, 1845

Wreathed in silk sheets and opium warmth, Cygnus' body lies inert. Above him— through him, in a sense— the Eye, his Eye, unveils its unsparing regard. Tonight, as Cygnus drowns in a stupor so deep it's nearly fatal, its gaze penetrates far and deep, farther and deeper than it ever has before. Broken mirror fragments blaze with razor light in a maelstrom of jagged, broken flashes.

…A vast necropolis, but nothing from Saqqara, nothing he has seen before. Stone after stone stretching to the edge of a green foothill. Behind the graves stands a mountain range with tall, narrow shoulders clad in snowy cerements…

...A warrior's face, half-ruined by a terrible scar and split by a grin of such ferocity and violence that it gleams like the blade of a sickle...

...A golden idol, horn raised, blazing with reflected sunlight against a red and glowering sky like a vast ocean of blood...

...A man— a sorcerer, Cygnus can sense, powerful and dangerous— stands clad in wind-ripped rags, one hand steadying himself upon the shoulder of a younger man with black hair like a crow's wing. The sorcerer's eyes, scorched and ruined, hide beneath a burlap blindfold. Beyond the two stretches a desert, vast, sunbaked, and dead. They are, he senses, at the beginning of a long and perilous journey...

...and for the first and only time that Cygnus can recall, the Eye recoils from what it has shown him, what it has seen.

He wakes bathed in sweat and turns his head just in time to vomit sour wine and philters into his nest of silk, befouling it. Cygnus can only half-recall the visions, and as consciousness cruelly reasserts itself within him, the fragments he can recall begin to slip away, leaving in their wake the dull awareness that he has taken too much tonight and poisoned himself with opium.

As the Eye withdraws, Cygnus calls for help.

Chapter One

Had the dead thing in the trap been a rabbit, once? It is hard to tell. The carcass—what is left of it—hasn't been touched by any scavengers save for the flies, which rise in extravagant, glittering clouds from its exposed entrails as Left Hand crouches over it.

It's as she thought.

The diseased animal (surely a rabbit, she thinks, looking at its long, twisted hind legs) would not have survived much longer, trap or no trap. She has seen this affliction in its final throes, when the beasts so plagued carry their entrails in a loose half-collapsed sack, a bloated, dangling bubble of guts that inevitably bursts, leaving the animal self-eviscer-ated and, after a time, dead. The rot is rife among the small animals and has begun to affect the larger game as well. The pollution is so noisome that Left Hand knows she may as well abandon the trap—or burn it. It has been irredeemably soiled, just like everything else that an animal so afflicted touches.

¤

Left Hand wakes at dawn, heralded by a brilliant, blood-red ribbon of light in the east that spreads until the entire sky is ablaze with crimson. When she pushes her way through the rounded entrance flap of the tipi, she almost gasps at the crisp morning air's contrast to the warm humidity sealed in-side. *Bad weather coming,* she thinks as she watches the dawn. She tries not to dwell on the ache that the wet and cold will bring to her hips: her joints are the least of her concerns re-garding the damp, given the fires on which she will rely to-day. She tastes the wind, drawing it deep into her sinuses and onto her tongue, and tries to judge the flavor of the rain and divine how long she has until it arrives. Long enough, she decides, or it will have to be, at any rate.

Mist wreaths the maples like smoke. Left Hand can feel the ghosts watching her from the shadows in the trees, and she can even see a few of the more adventurous (or confused) among their number. They stare at her with the black, empty sockets of their eyes until she loses her nerve and looks away. They won't bother her, she reminds herself, especially not in the performance of her duties this morning. Her efforts will be, after all, for their benefit as well as her own. She suspects that the evil plaguing her band has interfered with their repose, drawing them against their will from their endless sleep to stand here in the shadows of the maples, mute witnesses to the slow paring-down of their descendants' numbers.

Her band's encampment is not far from the clear, sweet streams that feed into the big water of the river. They follow the bison herd here every season. It was a hard winter, and one of Left Hand's sisters lost an infant to fever. It's usually a pleasure to return to the hunt in the spring; it ensures fresh meat, as well as something for bored and dispirited men to do to keep busy. But *this* spring has been different, proving, in fact, harder on their ranks than the winter. They've lost two braves and one elder thus far, which are more casualties than they'd seen in their last sortie against the Crow— and those sorties had been punishing enough. *These are grim reflections with which to begin a day*, she thinks and shakes her head as though to shed them like raindrops. Fretting isn't going to help matters; she's going to need her wits about her and more than a little luck.

Little Eagle is waiting for her near the banks of the stream. The other woman is swaddled in her thick buffalo robe, the fur collar of which stirs fitfully in the icy breeze blowing through the woods and off the water. She watches Left Hand thread her way through the tall grass to the sandy shore, where the bundles they've prepared in the preceding days wait for them. Little Eagle's eyes, Left Hand notes (as she does every time she sees them) are so dark they're almost black, as hard and bright as two chips of obsidian. Little Eagle, as Left Hand knows well, has seen a great many souls snuffed out and done the extinguishing herself on more than

10

one occasion. This bloodletting is reflected in her frank stare, and Left Hand is again glad that Little Eagle has joined the day's cause. Little Eagle's past— her family's slaughter at the hands of the Crow, her long stint as prisoner-wife to one of their warriors— is visible in the deep lines of her face and the tense set of her shoulders beneath the buffalo robe, but is likewise visible in the unforgiving iron of her gaze. Little Eagle, more than the braves Left Hand has known, has an unflinching and matter-of-fact approach to murder.

Left Hand isn't wearing a buffalo robe: she is clad in layers of soft leather. While she isn't as warm as Little Eagle looks, her movements are surprisingly fluid and relatively easy this morning despite her aches, which is blessing enough. She'll need her balance and cunning, both of which prove more difficult whenever her bones pain her too much. Little Eagle says nothing by way of greeting. When Left Hand reaches the shore of the stream, Little Eagle turns and draws a bundle wrapped in fur from the tall grass and hands it to her, then plucks a second one from the ground and lays it across her own shoulders. The two women pause for a moment with their packs and let their eyes play over the tree-line, drenched in mist, and the ghosts who linger there and stare mutely.

"Will they help us?" Little Eagle's voice is as flat as her eyes, but Left Hand can hear the fear in it nonetheless.

"No," Left Hand replies sadly. "They will not help us. The dead are no help to the living."

Little Eagle frowns. "That's not what we were taught. Not what the old man says."

"He loves pretty lies. He tells them to himself. And then to us."

Little Eagle grunts— whether in disgust at the unhelpful ghosts or the old man Left Hand isn't sure— and without another word trudges up the stream's bank and into the shadows of the maples. Left Hand follows behind her a few paces, and the two women begin their walk. The air riffles the surface of the stream and combs through the fur of Little Eagle's buffalo coat with frigid fingers. The change is gradual but noticeable. As the women follow the stream up a low hill choked with old maples, a stench begins to accompany the wind: an ammoniac, animal reek of blood and excrement. *We must be*, Left Hand decides, *on the right track.*

At the top of the hill, Little Eagle stops so abruptly that Left Hand, her eyes on her own trudging feet, nearly crashes into her. She stands stock-still, an eerie silhouette in her black robe until Left Hand comes abreast of her. "The dead are no help to the living?" she asks and points down the hill.

The ghosts that throng the hollow below the hill are as white as aspen trees, their eyes as black as night. There are so *many* of them, crowded into the shadows beneath the maples. All of them are pointing, their arms stretched longer than seems entirely human, their hands all converging with jagged fingers on a small cave entrance, out of which flows one of the tributary streams that will join the big river a few miles downstream. *Have we*, Left Hand wonders, *been drinking water that began its life here, in this cave of ghosts that smells like carrion*? The thought makes her guts turn a slow, greasy loop. Left Hand notes the silence; no birdsong, no sound of surreptitious movement in the underbrush, not even a breath of wind, now, to stir the dry maple leaves. Even the little stream barely makes a whisper as it slips past a berm of slimy rocks. There is only silence and the stench of death, thick and meaty.

And the ghosts.

"Ignore them," Left Hand whispers and shrugs the bundle off her shoulder gently to the ground. "Just do as we planned— and hope that we won't be joining their ranks today."

The branches of the maples surrounding the cave entrance are dry despite the stream that flows nearby, but Little Eagle is still able to find enough young, green boughs to build a large, smoky fire near the cave entrance. She works in silence and stokes the flame low so that the wood is consumed slowly and generates big, billowing clouds of thick white smoke. As Little Eagle is tending to this task, Left Hand unpacks their bundles. They contain gourds, each sealed with a cork, which give a pregnant slosh as Left Hand lines them up on the ground. She draws a flint knife from her belt and sets to work on a handful of long, thick branches selected by Little Eagle for this purpose. Before long, she has fashioned

14

an armful of stout, simple spears, which she sharpens to needle points.

Although the women labor in silence, each focused on her task, Left Hand can tell that some question must be burning in Little Eagle's throat, aching to be voiced. At length, she finally speaks up. "How do you know to use fire? The one that Tall Elk chased off— he stabbed it enough times to have turned its guts to slush. And it endured. How can you know *this* will work?"

Left Hand looks up from her work and squints at Little Eagle. "You ask me this *now*?"

Little Eagle almost seems embarrassed. "I didn't think to ask until now. I suppose it doesn't make a difference."

Left Hand is quiet for a moment as she weighs her words. "A dream," she says finally. "Thunder spoke to me in a dream and told me what to do. I woke, and once I was awake, Thunder spoke to me again. His voice was so loud it almost split my skull. I suspect He wanted to be sure I understood, that I didn't forget or confuse the dream." She pauses, unsure of how much to reveal, but the words come tumbling out of her

15

like heavy stones ripping through the bottom of a rotted-out basket. "I suspect that He decided to intervene because He knows that we cannot afford to lose any more people, and, for all our differences, neither can the Crow. And we cannot keep fighting the Crow. What they want, I understand— you, of all people, understand best. They want game, they want glory. Sometimes, they want wives. Tell me— what do the wašíču want?" Little Eagle shrugs.

"The wašíču," Left Hand continues, "the white men? They hunger. For land, always land, but game, too. And most of all, death. They hunger for it, and in their hunger, they even eat their god."

"I have heard this. They *really* eat their god?"

Left Hand nods. "His flesh, and they drink his blood. Can you imagine what they want to do to us? We must survive. And we're going to need the Crow, just as we're going to need every single one of our band, all those men and women and children still asleep warm back at the camp."

"We're going to need more than that," Little Eagle says, studying the tree line where the ghosts have begun to fade

16

like melting mist in the rising light of dawn. "We're going to need our dead, as well. All the help we can muster."

Left Hand considers this for a moment and looks into the gloom at the edge of the trees. The ghosts have all vanished but one, a lonely sentinel standing in the few remaining shadows, still stretching its slender, too-long arm to point at the cave mouth. "You are most likely right," she says finally.

Little Eagle nods, and after that, the women work in silence until the spears are ready and the fire's smoke, concentrated near the mouth of the cave, is almost too thick for them to breathe. Left Hand plucks one of the liquid-filled gourds from the stack at her feet. She pulls the cork free from its neck and lobs it underhand into the mouth of the cave, where it splashes its contents against the rocks and rolls into the darkness. She repeats this process with each gourd until the rocky throat of the cave is painted with great, oily fans of the fluid, which gives off fumes so potent that they make the air above the entrance shimmer. The kerosene had been the hardest part of the preparations that Left Hand had made. It had taken her months to trade with the wašíču for it. A chemical aroma that now rises from the cave and adds its bouquet to the death-smell and the smoke. No disasters have struck thus far, and she allows herself a moment of hope that her hard work and planning will prevail on this day.

Left Hand approaches the fire and selects a branch whose thick end juts, intact, from the blaze. She lifts the burning branch and tosses it carefully at the cave mouth. The effect is instantaneous and spectacular. The makeshift torch doesn't even touch the rocks before the kerosene's fumes ignite with a tremendous *whoosh* and a gout of flame. The fire swiftly races down the throat of the cave, throwing fitful light against the thick curtain of smoke from the burning branches. Left Hand remembers the voice of Thunder as He had instructed her on how to build the walls of fire and smoke. *Trap them*, He had said, *between suffocation and the inferno. Cleanse them with fire, scour the impurity from where it hides. They are a sickness. They will continue to plague My people until you do this thing for Me.*

Left Hand doesn't stop at one branch. She snatches a handful of them from the bonfire one at a time and hurls them into the cave, where they fall like crackling comets and add to the fire already blazing there. The rocky gullet of the cave has become an inferno.

The cacophony starts with a single shriek, which rises from the stone teeth of the cave as though the earth itself has begun to scream. The soloist is joined by other voices almost immediately, and before long, the burning cave gives voice to a hellish chorus of high-pitched, atonal agony. There is nothing human in the sound— indeed, nothing even recognizably animal. It is, Left Hand decides immediately, the most awful thing she has ever heard. Had Little Eagle not been there, Left Hand knows that she would flee. Whatever curse she had thought she was prepared to face, this is worse by far than anything she had imagined. Little Eagle's black eyes show no fear, though— just disgust and something else, something cold that Left Hand suspects might be the murder lurking in her heart. Little Eagle, she realizes, has come to this task equipped with something that Left Hand lacks: the same hunger for death that burns in the wašíču.

She has come to deal death, and to die.

Little Eagle takes a spear in each hand and wraps her fin-

19

gers so tightly that her knuckles turn white. The needle tips point steadily at the burning mouth of the cave. Left Hand follows her example and readies her own spears, although her spear-points, unlike Little Eagle's, jig and jag shakily. Both women have an arsenal of backup spears at their feet, which Left Hand has a sinking feeling that they will need. When Left Hand looks at Little Eagle a second time, trying to draw some courage from her sister-in-arms, she can hardly believe her eyes. Little Eagle's usually-funereal face is split by a huge grin, a frightening thing that shows so many teeth that it's nearly a snarl. Even more strangely, Left Hand doesn't feel put off by it. She actually feels a bit braver. Little Eagle, she thinks, is exactly where she wants to be right now. I should count myself lucky to kill and die beside her.

Spears in hand and hunger for death ignited, Left Hand and Little Eagle ready themselves and begin to wait.

They do not have to wait long.

Charles Bernard

Part I: 1848

Chapter Two

"I'm fair starved," says Abner as the graveyard comes into view, "and we've spent our daylight. I suggest we stop." The steady tread of horses and an occasional muffled knock or a metallic jingle from the pack behind him provides a musical counterpart to his words: slow timpani drums and the hint of a harp, perhaps.

"When we've been making such good time?" his brother replies. Miles' tone is serious, but his eyes glint like two mischievous chips of ice, blue above his black beard. "Look yonder, Ab, and go fetch yourself a leg of mutton from out the boneyard if you're so famished. Sure, but the fellow you take it from won't need it again until Gabriel sounds his trumpet, and since you're no doubt damned for your gluttony, you may as well indulge."

"He'll have his brother's company at the devil's table," says Leonidas. Both men turn in their saddles at the sound of their father's voice, deep and sure as stone. "Though, even if you be damned for sloth, I don't doubt you'll be asleep there at your plate, flames or no." They both grin at this, and the grins bear the stamp of their mother's feature so clearly that Leonidas feels his heart break for the thousandth time since her death. *I could cross this entire continent,* he thinks, *indeed, I am crossing it, but there will be no escape from this grief. How could there be, when I carry it with me?*

"There'll be no mutton," he adds. He ruminates for a moment. "Hmmm. It's passing strange— a graveyard nestled here. A big graveyard. I haven't marked another living man today, nor yesterday. Now we've marked a veritable village—of the dead. No matter; we'll stop to make camp once we're nearer the river. It shouldn't be far now." Leonidas' prediction is accurate. Just over the next rise, the Pyburn men find a broad, shallow slope, and strewn upon it like a frayed and muddy scarf lies the Missouri River. Its surface is as flat as an iron. A fertile estuary funk, marshy and alive, drifts in and out of perceptibility as the wind breaths over the water. The breeze is cool, the setting sun warm, and the evening alive with the drone of crickets and the river's raucous congress of buntings, tanagers, and grosbeaks. The Pyburns prepare their night's camp on a soft patch of level ground that overlooks a bend in the Missouri.

Miles tends to the horses, and Leonidas builds a fire as Abner fetches water. The chores are rote, the roles familiar, even at this early point in their journey. Thus far the trip has gone more smoothly than the men had any right to hope. *Once wagons and dependents are pared away*, Leonidas muses, *perhaps the trip to California is not as daunting as popular wisdom in Illinois would have it*. The Pyburns have no more with them than the clothing they wear—new boots, linen shirts, and black trousers— and what their horses can carry. And, of course, Leonidas has brought the letter, carefully folded and re-folded so many times that the paper is like velvet. He has pored over it enough to have committed the salient portion to memory:

You & my nephews must come quick as you can. If this claim proves as rich as it seems, will be too much labor for one & I would prefer that my sister's sons see the profits & not strangers. Come partner with me, Leonidas, & make our fortunes.

The last dregs of sunset stain the sky as the three Pyburn men settle into the evening's mellow contemplations. Leonidas stirs a pot of beans every so often as it bubbles over the fire and watches his sons distract themselves in their own ways, each as different as their faces are alike. Abner reads his Bible by firelight. His lips move as he struggles through his evening's selection. Despite his devout faith and love of his holy book, his reading has always been a struggle, and the words on the page come clumsily to him despite years of effort. Miles, on the other hand, had a fine mind for letters, although he had never cared for books as much as he had for boxing (and less organized, more extracurricular pugilism). He sings to himself now as he feeds long twigs into the fire. His voice is low and melodious. The song is one that Leonidas recognizes as a favorite of his late wife's, one she had sung to Miles and Abner unnumbered times.

Full dark falls thick and close. It surrounds the three Pyburn men like a wool blanket. Leonidas enjoys this, enjoys the erasure of all things but the golden circle of firelight, the somnolent sound of the horses' breath, and the perfume of wood smoke. Just as the day's tension is beginning to release its claws from Leonidas' shoulders and back, Miles pauses his singing to clear his throat and lick his lips. When he does, there is a moment of deep quiet in which the pop of the fire and the whisper of the river are the loudest sounds. Just as Miles draws breath to resume his song, a sound splits the night like a hook ripping through flesh.

When Leonidas was young, his father had taken him to see a two-headed lamb that had been born on a farm in a neighboring town. The poor, doomed creature had lived for less than a year before expiring. The farmer had offered them a dark prediction about what the birth may have been an omen of (a notion in which neither Leonidas nor his father put much stock) and led them to the hay-strewn corner of his barn where the unfortunate creature passed its days. The lamb did not have two fully formed heads, which is what Leonidas had imagined. Instead, it had one misshapen head marred by two monstrous half-faces that were squashed to-gether in a nauseating portmanteau: three eyes, two muzzles, and a heart-shaped skull crowned by two bulbous domes. The sight alone was near enough to make Leonidas vomit, but then, it had opened its truncated muzzles and given vent to a sound that echoed in his nightmares for months. It had voiced a flat, blatting moan, somewhere between the moan of a sick animal and the cry of a human child. Its distorted sinuses had given the sound a piercing, reedy quality that he could feel in his bones.

The call that reverberates in the air now has some of that lamb's cry to it, but it is louder, deeper, and filled with an anguished rage that is distressing in both its proximity to a human voice and its unmistakably animal timbre. Leonidas feels gooseflesh rise on his arms and the nape of his neck. The horses, hitherto resting in sleepy quietude, shake their heads and whinny in fear. Miles and Abner glance at their father, then at each other—their mannerisms so alike in that moment they could be twins— and, without needing to consult Leonidas or each other, silently pull themselves to their feet and collect their rifles. When the call comes a second time, the horses panic. Abner hurries to calm them as they rear and stamp and soon has them under control, though they continue to whinny and toss their heads.

"That was closer." Miles sounds calm, but the flickering firelight refuses to hide the unease on his face.

"Hmm," agrees Leonidas. He rests his own rifle in the crook of his arm, glad of its weight. He and Miles both stand, backs to the fire, and face the direction from which the call had sounded in the darkness. Back in the direction from which they had come— toward the cemetery.

"Bear? Wildcat?"

"Hmm," Leonidas replies.

"Had more the flavor of the human, did it not?" asks Abner. The horses soothed, he joins his father and brother, back to the fire, eyes on the total darkness beyond the shivering ring of firelight.

Leonidas is about to reply when a shape stumbles out of the darkness, white as a sheet and waving its arms as it blunders toward the Pyburns. All three men lift their rifles, but before the night can be split by fire and lead, the shape emerges from shadow. It's a man, ghost-pale and clad in a stained white linen shirt and tan, dirty trousers. His eyes are wide and wild, and his right arm is bloody from elbow to fingertip.

"Heavenly Father, help us," the man gasps and sinks to his knees. "Please, sirs, we must…"

His voice trails into a whisper, then stops. The man's eyes roll to the whites, and he collapses to the earth insensate.

¤

"Something's been at him," says Miles.

"Mmm," agrees Leonidas, inspecting the man's truncated right hand. All of the fingers but the index and thumb have been reduced to ragged stumps. To his eyes, the injury doesn't look like it was made by a blade. It looks like the work of teeth. Dull teeth. "Fetch me twine and a clout."

Leonidas binds the man's hand in a rag, which soon darkens to a damp red, but the bleeding slows. Abner and Miles carefully move the unconscious man nearer the fire, where its warmth can restore a portion of his vitality. Blood loss or distress— or both— have turned the fellow as white as snow. "Coffee," Leonidas says to Abner, and his son dutifully sets to the task while the Pyburns' unexpected visitor mutters in his uneasy stupor. As the percolator bubbles, Leo slaps the man lightly, bringing a touch of color back to his cheeks and the light of waking thought to his eyes.

"Oh, thank you, gentlemen, this is surely providence! Surely! Please, we must—that is, with *four* of us…" He pauses, then: "I forget myself. Will you pray with me?"

"Were you attacked?" asks Miles. "Bobcat?"

"Miles," admonishes his father. Then, "We'll pray."

The Pyburns bow their heads with the man, whose name, they learn, is Christiansen. After they pray, Miles retrieves a flat pint bottle from his pack and waggles it at their guest. "Whisky?"

"No, thank you," says Christiansen, and Leonidas nods approvingly. Abner offers the man coffee, which he also refuses (an abstention which Leonidas finds somewhat less comprehensible) in favor of water, a bowl of beans, and a blanket draped over his narrow shoulders. For a time, none of the men speak. The fire casts its undulating light onto their faces: Leonidas weathered and sharp-featured, Abner narrow-mouthed with worry etched upon his forehead, Miles with his coal-black beard and dancing eyes. And this newcomer, Christiansen, whose limp gray-and-white hair and deeply lined features give him an air of exhausted haplessness as he chews his beans and tries to gather his thoughts.

After a quiet in which the pop of the fire and the creak of the crickets are the loudest sounds, Leonidas clears his throat. "Christiansen?" he asks. The old man sighs, and the tale seeps out of him like blood oozing from a shallow cut.

He'd been a sexton, first in his native Stockholm and then in Ohio, where he had immigrated with his wife. There, the Christiansens had encountered followers of the charismatic young prophet, Joseph Smith. Christiansen— formerly a Church of Sweden Lutheran— had been swept up in a wave of religious awakening and had converted, convinced that

32

Smith was a communicant with the divine and had been selected by the Almighty to restore His church in North America, which was the true promised land. The last five years had proven to be a trial for the nascent Mormon religion and for the aging couple. First, Smith's followers had been expelled from one territory after another; then came the assassination of the prophet at the hands of a mob. "So," Christiansen says and flaps one hand disinterestedly in the direction the sun fled, "we go west."

Hardship had not yet eaten its fill of the Mormons, however. Brigham Young, the faith's new leader, led them as far as Nebraska Territory the previous year. There, the band of pioneers had established Winter Quarters, a temporary settlement of tents and log cabins near the Missouri River. It had been a bitter winter and a costly one. All told, Young lost almost three hundred souls before spring came. The Latter-Day Saints— as the faithful styled themselves— had died of blackleg and malaria, childbirth and misadventure. Christiansen the sexton had been tasked with laying out and digging the graves of the departed in the mysterious cemetery that the Pyburns had passed earlier that evening. "Come spring," Christiansen says, "most went on to find Zion. I stayed."

"Why?" asks Abner. His tone is gentle.

"To bury my wife," Christiansen replies. "At least, that's why I stayed at first."

He discovered the first desecration a few days after the main group of emigrants had left Winter Quarters. "It was an affront. Graves dug up. Bits of my brethren mixed together. Bits of them missing." He was flummoxed. He knew his trade and had sunk every grave in the cemetery a good six feet into the soft, heavy earth. "Most men, they dig graves a meter deep. Not me. Always two meters. Upon the return of the Lord, we shall be clad again in our flesh, so we must treat the dead with respect. Though He shall provide the restitution of all things, of course." Be that as it may, Christiansen had reinterred what remains he could, packing the dirt down as hard as possible. The next morning, he'd been drawn by a stench to a grave in another corner of the cemetery that had suffered the same fate: dug up, the body ripped from its shroud and mauled.

Miles' mouth puckers in disgust. "Vile. Did you get a look at any tracks?"

"Oh, yes," replies Christiansen, "there were tracks." They had been difficult to miss in the loose scattering of displaced soil. Had, in fact, been pressed so clearly into the ground that it was almost as though what had left them had wanted to eliminate any possibility of mistaking their nature.

They had been unmistakably human prints, made by a barefoot pair of long, slender feet. Leonidas feels a chill climb his back despite the warmth of the fire. "I had no choice then," says Christiansen with a sigh. "I reburied the remaining portions of the dead, armed myself as best as I could with a shovel and a lantern, and I stood watch over the graves of my neighbors." His efforts had been rewarded—if you could call it that— that very night.

"I followed the sound of digging. Grave robbers, I thought. I'd heard tell of resurrectionists back where I come from, but we are far from student doctors here, are we not? Maybe some of the Omaha, I thought then. But I was wrong."

35

Christiansen shivers and stares into the fire with wide, un-blinking eyes for a few moments, then continues his recount-ing.

"It was naked. Naked among the dead and… eating of them. I thought at first it was a man— a madman, to be sure, but a man. I raised the lantern and beheld it clearly, and knew it to be no man." He'd bellowed and swung the shovel, but the thing was stronger than it looked— "long-boned and unwholesome" is how he describes it— and had fought back. He had dropped his lantern grappling with it, and the strug-gle was thus illuminated sporadically and from a strange angle. Its slack mouth had concealed a bouquet of jagged, half-broken teeth, and it had delivered a bite that had lain waste to his right hand. "Please, will you help?" Christiansen waves his hand, swaddled in Leonidas' makeshift bandage. "I'm afraid I do not think that I can surmount it on my own, and my wife's grave, I do not think I could bear…" His voice trails off in a disconsolate trickle.

What transpires next occurs quickly and in the silent, timeworn shorthand of deep familial ties. Abner and Miles share a glance in which amusement, unease, and youthful impatience with the nonsense of old men blend into a wordless accord: *Quite a campfire tale, old-timer. Now off with you.* A scant half-second later, the boys meet their father's stare, in which there is reprimand and sharp reproach: *Hold your tongues, callow boys. This is my decision, and I will brook no argument.* Though none of this is said aloud, all is clearly and quickly conveyed in the lexicon of deep ancestral familiarity. The only words that are said aloud are spoken by Leonidas: "We'll come have a look."

¤

The cemetery isn't far. The men walk single file led by Miles, who carries a rifle and a torch that lights the way with dancing yellow half-light. His brother follows closely behind, his own rifle in the crook of his arm. The two bicker amiably in low voices as they walk. Behind them is Christiansen, followed by Leonidas, who carries a torch, his own rifle, and something tucked into his waistband in case of real trouble— something that sits heavy and cold against his hip. He's tired; the day was long before the old man showed up with his bloody hand and wild tale. The voices of his sons, clear and strong, make Leonidas feel proud as always, true. But the endless tide of hungry youth that washes forever forward long ago left him behind. He sees the slump in Christiansen's shoulders and his leaden tread and imagines that he must feel the same— much worse, actually. Christiansen's wife was gone now, and his people had quite *literally* left him behind with the dead as they'd gone on in search of their promised land.

"Your people that moved on," Leonidas says, "and you, you're Mormons?"

Christiansen starts as though stuck with a pin, then answers after a moment's hesitation. "Yes. You've heard of our movement? Our Prophet?"

"In Nauvoo. There was quite the uproar over his revelations."

"An uproar," says Christiansen mildly, "I suppose you could call it that, yes."

"Mmm." Christiansen seems weary and sickly. The stubs of his subtracted fingers must be giving him more grief than it seemed at first, Leonidas figures. Something more seems required of him, and he speaks up after another long moment's silence. "I heard about what happened to your Prophet in Carthage. That wasn't right. A mob's a mindless thing." He feels there's more to be said, but after struggling to put more of his feelings into words, all he manages is: "A mob's a cowardly thing, too."

Ahead of them on the trail, Miles and Abner have stopped walking and stand, shoulder-to-shoulder. Miles lifts his torch and calls back cheerfully over his shoulder, "We've arrived!"

Christiansen and the men of Winter Quarters planted their modest cemetery in the midst of a stand of maple trees, set back a piece from the river but near enough to it that the water's murmur can be heard beneath the music of the crickets. The earth beneath Leonidas' boots is soft, almost spongy— the sort of earth that takes a grave well. He knows from the ones he's dug himself. There was his mother, back in New York, followed in short order by his father. He'd buried a wife and a daughter. He knows a bit about burying the dead— enough to see, even in the uneven torchlight, that

Christiansen the sexton had plied his craft with meticulous attention to detail.

The graves are evenly spaced, laid out in straight lines whose orderliness stands in mute contrast to the tall maples and their riotous undergrowth. There are a lot of them. How many had Christiansen said they'd lost that winter, three hundred? Each is adorned by a simple wooden marker, and in the dim and shifting light, Leonidas thinks that they look like strange crops: a small farm's worth of petrified corn-stalks, perhaps. The winter must have seemed interminable. He imagines the Latter-Day Saints huddled in their tents and cabins, watching loved ones sicken, waiting for the long, fro-zen darkness of the season to pass so that the search for the Promised Land might resume.

"It was over this way," Christiansen says, stepping past Miles and Abner. His tongue seems to have thickened and grown sluggish, and he slurs his words as he speaks. The wound, Leonidas thinks again, must be bothering him some-thing fierce. Miles follows a pace behind Christiansen, his step jaunty and untroubled, but Abner hangs back a moment and addresses his father in a low voice. "Father, please excuse me for saying so, but this seems ill-advised."

"Hmmm?"

"That fellow is sickly. And something here feels... unclean."

Leonidas feels it , too: a coiled and curdled repulsion in the pit of his stomach that is incongruous with the peaceful graves and their simple markers. He can tell from Miles' jaunty stride and the casual way his rifle is cozied in the crook of his arm that he doesn't have the same misgivings, nor, it is evident, does he believe a word of the old man's wild tale.

Miles' high spirits evaporate immediately when they come upon the first desecrated grave.

It takes Leonidas a moment to realize what lies before them, strewn with jubilant abandon about the ruins of the violated grave. He thinks it might be the half-eaten carcass of a rabbit, or maybe a fawn, but no. The light gleams off the bony curve of a well-chewed skull, and he realizes that this had been a child. His guts roil, and his hand tightens on the stock of his rifle. He steels himself and steps closer to the grave, holding his light aloft. Just as Christiansen said, the soft earth disturbed by the haphazard exhumation is rife with bare human footprints— footprints that are *almost* human, at any rate, but unnatural in their slender length.

Miles is the first to speak up, his voice brittle with shock. "Who in God's name would—"

Before he can finish his question, the night's chorus of crickets and frog song is split by a terrible sound. It's the same ruined-lamb moan that soiled the evening earlier but colored more by delight this time than anger. "I believe," says Leonidas, "we are near to finding out." The Pyburns check their rifles in the gloom as Christiansen stares without blinking at the grisly tickertape tatters of meat that litter the ground around the yawning idiot mouth of the disinterred grave. Leonidas doesn't care for the way the scattered torchlight pools in Christiansen's eyes, nor for the wet set of his lips. He prods the old man in the ribs with the butt of his rifle, perhaps a touch harder than necessary. Christiansen snaps back to attention as though awakened from a doze.

"Yes," he says, "please, let us hurry!"

They come upon the creature as it is freeing another body from its grave at the edge of the cemetery, where the neat lines of markers border the deep darkness of the thickest stands of maples. *"Long-boned and unwholesome,"* thinks Leonidas, *is that how Christiansen had described it*? The words are apt. The thing looks like a terrible imitation of a human, one with limbs unnaturally long and asymmetrically twisted, its posture ruined and painful-looking. When they come upon it, the thing has a mouth full of meat and an expression of vacant ecstasy on its terrible, puckered face. Its long, bone-slender fingers terminate in thick, ragged nails— claws, really— that are black with unspeakable grime. Its skin is so pale that it would practically glow in the darkness were the thing's hide not obscured by a layer of grave dirt. A few wisps of long white hair cling to its skull. It's completely naked and unmistakably male and seems utterly unconcerned with the sudden presence of Christiansen or the Pyburns. As Leonidas watches, numb with revulsion, it frees a long, glistening ribbon of meat from the innards of the body it is crouched upon. It sucks this dainty between its smeared lips with much evident relish, to judge by its slurping and smacking. In the torchlight, the gore that paints its mouth looks as black as ink.

Abner takes the first shot without hesitating. It misses the mark completely, and he barks an oath that proves that he can blaspheme with as much fervor as his brother when the situation warrants. Miles stands rigid and gawps at the thing, his rifle forgotten and clutched rigidly between his fists.

"MILES!" Leonidas roars, but the younger man is as motionless as a statue, petrified by shock, or fear, or both. The creature flinches when Abner's shot whines past it and whirls around with a snarl in which Leonidas can hear a terribly *human* anger— but no fear. It regards the three men with glazed, milky eyes and lifts its lip, baring its jagged teeth. The rifle in Leonidas' hands roars before he's even aware that he has lifted it to his shoulder, let alone squeezed the trigger. His shot is surer than Abner's, but at the very moment he fires, the thing lunges, and what might have been a lethal shot instead clips the creature's flesh just above its jutting, crooked collarbone. The shot leaves a strangely bloodless wound. If the thing feels any pain at its injury, it gives no sign.

Christiansen, meanwhile, has fallen to his knees in the dirt beside a second desecrated grave. It had housed the body of a woman, now pulled from the earth after what must have been a riot of digging, judging by the disheveled soil. She has been ripped free from both shroud and clothing from the waist up, exposing breasts withered by hunger and sickness. Her face has been chewed away and her belly torn open, and her guts are strewn merrily about. Christiansen's back is to Leonidas, his shoulders hunched and rigid. *He's unmanned. Quite the hunting party we've turned out to be*, Leonidas thinks. *Half our number have proved entirely useless, and the other half not much better.*

All of this transpires in a handful of moments, as though time has turned to molasses. The thing— *perhaps endowed with reasoning*, Leonidas thinks, *who knows?* — seems aware that their bungling has supplied it with an unexpected advantage. It lunges for Miles' throat with its rotting fangs. Before it can deliver its bite, however, Abner swings his rifle at it barrel-first and connects with a lucky shot to its ribs. The blow doubles it over, but only for a moment. When it raises its head and fixes its eyes on Abner, forgetting Miles, there is no way to mistake the look in its eyes: a very palpable, very human hatred.

The thing wheels around and grapples with Abner, who grunts with surprise and effort—for all the twisted misalignment of its elongated and lopsided skeleton, it is possessed of an intense and febrile strength. It looks almost as though the two are dancing, wrapped as tightly as any lovers. Miles' trance breaks, and he drops his torch, bringing his rifle up to his shoulder. The torch lights the struggle between Abner and the thing from below and casts weird, writhing shadows that are pushed back for a moment as Miles' rifle roars and emits a long plume of flame. Miles' shot smacks into the thing's bony back with an audible *thwap,* and it grunts in surprise and pain. Enraged, the thing darts its head forward and sinks its fangs into Abner. It tries for his throat, but Abner pulls away, and its jaws close on the thick meat of his shoulder instead. It's a deep, vicious bite and elicits a howl of pain. *Well,* Leonidas thinks, *things have gone about as badly as they could have.* There's no time to reload the rifle, so he drops it, closes the distance to the thing, grips one of its misshapen arms, and— wishing fervently he were a praying man—reaches for his waistband.

In preparation for the trip West to join his brother-in-law, Leonidas had purchased only what he considered the bare essentials. His thinking had been that light travel makes fast travel, and the quicker the Pyburn men could get to California, the better. The missive from his brother-in-law, the one that had prompted this trip to begin with, had counseled that they make haste and travel safely. Leonidas was not a dweller or a fretter by nature, but the prospect of crossing an entire continent had twisted his guts into a burning knot of anxiety, and so he had visited a gunsmith and made what was, for him, an extravagant purchase.

The Whitneyville Hartford Dragoon Revolver weighs five pounds and is more than a foot long. It's still so new that the glimmer of its silver finish in the firelight is a thing of cold and elegant beauty. Leonidas had not purchased it for its beauty, but because though the contraption takes more than five minutes to reload using his still-inexperienced fingers, it does not require long to fire. This is a fact Leonidas now demonstrates in a maelstrom of lead and flame. He pulls the creature close and squeezes off all six shots in rapid succession. This fusillade is delivered at near-point-blank range into the thing's emaciated guts. The effect is instantaneous and ruinous: the hail of fire blows long, red-purple ropes of intestine out the thing's back, nearly bisecting it. The dim light of noisome life leaves its eyes, and it slumps to the stained dirt, dead and as hollowed out as the body of a cello. In the ruins of its guts, tossed about the grave dirt, Leonidas can see the half-digested scraps of its midnight banquet: here a finger, there a bite of face or organ meat. He allows himself one moment's struggle with his gorge, and then, victory won over his nausea, he turns to his sons.

Chapter Three

The sweet smell of expended gunpowder hangs in the air, nearly as thick as the stench of rotting flesh. The copper tang of blood is subtler, but its presence is unmistakable as well. Whatever hellish light had been present in the thing's cloudy eyes has been extinguished. Leonidas can't imagine it rising from the earth to do more mischief, given that the entire totality of the thing's innards is now scattered from hell to breakfast over the uneven surface of the excavated graves. Even so, he kicks its ruined corpse experimentally, Dragoon still leveled at its head. When it flops limply in place at his prodding, still quite dead, Leonidas presses the Dragoon roughly into Miles' hands and shoves him out of the way. He snatches his torch from where it lies burning on the ground and rushes to tend to Abner, casting what light he can onto Abner's wound.

It's deep and nasty and bleeds freely, soaking Abner's shirt. For having such a paltry-looking set of jaws and such rotten, broken teeth, the misshapen grave-robber had, Leonidas thinks, delivered one hell of a bite. That said, the wound hardly seems life-threatening. "What in God's name *was* that thing?" Miles asks as he angrily turns to interrogate Christiansen, forgotten by the Pyburns in the chaos of unexpected mortal combat.

Christiansen rests on his knees beside one of the desecrated graves. He has not moved so much as a digit since the beginning of the tumult. "Christiansen?" Leonidas asks and lifts his torch nearer to the Latter Day Saint. The old man's face bears a look of horror that is transcendent, almost sublime. Above his twisted mouth, his cloudy eyes stare sightlessly into the darkness of the violated grave. *Were those eyes*, Leonidas asks himself, *this milky in life*? It's hard to remember. When Leonidas tries, all he can think about is the howl that Abner had loosed when the thing bit him and how its guts had sprayed out its violated back at the touch of his Dragoon. Leonidas bends to shake Christiansen's shoulder and verify what he suspects. Yes, indeed, at some point the excitement or the horror of the confrontation with the grave-robbing scavenger had proven too much for him. As Leonidas bends toward the old man, he spies the name on the marker denoting the exhumed grave of the partially devoured woman.

Eufenia Christiansen

1789 – 1848

Alskade Fru

Leonidas feels a chill run up his spine like an icy centipede. Christiansen's heart must have given out at the sight of his wife's body, naked and defiled. Leonidas feels a swell of pity for the man, despite the bitter outcome of his intrusion on the Pyburn camp: this unwanted, unwarranted nightmare of death and corruption. Miles' throat, nearly torn out. Poor Abner's shoulder, shredded by the rotten maw of that horri-

51

ble thing. "Go get the shovels."

Miles is incredulous. "Good *God*, Father. Can't that wait until morning? Look at Abner: he's *bleeding*."

"Then he will rest, and we will work. We will not leave this place befouled, Miles. I don't cotton to their self-declared prophet's ridiculous religious fantasies, but Christiansen certainly did. From what I remember of their theology, funerary disposition is important to them. They believe that they shall stand before the Lord upon His return, clad in the flesh and cerements in which they were laid to rest."

"You're not telling me that you believe any of that charlatan's—"

"*Listen* to me when I'm talking, boy!" Leonidas snarls, and Miles' jaw closes so suddenly that his teeth click audibly together. "Of *course*, I don't believe any of their nonsense, any more than the nonsense spewed by that water-headed fellow your mother loved so much."

"Jabez Swan?"

"That's the one. I believe that dead's dead. A man draws his last breath, and then it is dirt and darkness and dissolution, and nothing more. But *he* believed in eternal progression, and we'll pay him no disrespect after his death." Leonidas sighs. "Now, seeing as you couldn't screw your cowardly guts in place long enough to protect your brother, can you at least spare me your argument and go. Fetch. The. Shovels?"

Stung, Miles turns without a word and stalks off in the direction of the Pyburn camp.

"Come here, boy." Leonidas' voice is firm, but his fingers are gentle as he probes Abner's bite. The thing's rotten fangs left a wide ring of uneven punctures, and the skin surrounding the wound is already beginning to bruise and swell. The loss of blood has slowed, and by the time that Miles returns with a pair of shovels, the bleeding has stopped entirely, and the shallower pocks have begun to scab over. Even so, Leonidas insists that Abner sit while his brother and father work to return the graves to order and to bury Christiansen.

Miles and Leonidas wordlessly agree to each work alone. Miles' pride has been bruised by Leonidas' words, and his father, for his part, is happy for the excuse not to apologize

53

for his anger. They are both aware that it's pure luck that neither Abner nor Miles lost his life during the course of the evening's horrors. The work of reassembling the graves is solitary, filthy, and performed in the rippling half-shadows of the meager torchlight. Leonidas sets to work returning Eufenia to her shroud; he notes with detached interest that the cerements of her burial are quite complex. He first returns her exposed, violated torso to what he can only think of as vaguely Masonic undergarments, made of heavy, unbleached cotton and marked with a reverse-L shaped symbol on the right breast, a V-shaped symbol or glyph on the right breast, and a horizontal slash over the belly (*over where her belly* should *be*, Leonidas thinks). Over these undergarments, Eufenia had been buried in a long white dress, white stockings, and white shoes, all of which were soiled with grave dirt (and other stains that Leonidas preferred not to speculate about). He returns her remains to these layers as best as he can. Although Leonidas would never admit to it even if tortured, he feels a dull thrill of excitement in his loins as he lays his hands on Eufenia's cold, bare flesh, her dead, withered breasts with their purple, mottled skin and rough nipples. It is the first time that Leonidas has touched a woman's bare flesh since the death of his wife, and for months after this awful night, he will lie awake at times, thinking of the feel of the dead woman's breasts in his hands. The memory is to become like an oily stain in his mind, one that will prove difficult to wash away.

It is in this state, roiling with disgust at himself and grappling with a persistent nervous pleasure that inflames his loins, that Leonidas spies a glimmer of gold in the loose dirt at the edge of Eufenia's grave. He bends and plucks a heavy object from the soil. He shakes it free of dirt. After a glance over his shoulder to confirm that Miles' back is to him, he slips it into his pocket. It's an impulsive act, performed almost without any conscious thought at all, but the weight of the trinket grows as he returns Eufenia to her soiled burial gown and then to the remnants of her coffin. He hesitates. *We've done this much. What's a little lump of gold?* The magnanimous Leonidas, the wise father (as he sometimes fancied himself) had insisted that they help Christiansen, and then

55

had further insisted that they toil here in the rancid night, cleaning up the aftermath. The West, it would seem, did not favor such a man. *To hell with it*, he thinks. *Gold or the grave; if it's to be one or the other out here, I know which path is mine.*

Whatever Christiansen's beliefs, the Pyburns are only able to do so much. Leonidas and Miles converge on the old man's body, which is heavier than it looks and weighs more than his wife's by far. Together, father and son drag the older man to his wife's grave. At least, Leonidas observes, Christiansen had been wearing his own sacred undergarments during the evening's events. He can therefore be buried in them, albeit bereft of a shroud or his own coffin. They reunite the Christiansens in the remains of Eufenia's coffin.

"That thing had the strength of the devil in it," the usually skeptical Miles notes as he stares at the shattered lid of the coffin. It had to have been brought with the ill-fated pioneers. It was simple, but it was oak, crafted with attention to detail, and was stout. *What kind of man brings a coffin with him on his trip to the Promised Land?* Leonidas thinks, then answers his own question: *A sextant does.*

"It tore its way in as if it were opening a pantry door," he agrees. Working together, Leonidas and Miles lay the Christiansens to bed beneath the soft, black earth to await the Resurrection.

The creature is another matter. Its denuded spine and sodden innards remind Leonidas of tinned fish, and he has to struggle, again, not to vomit. He makes Miles drag it out beyond the edge of the graveyard; between its twisted, emaciated limbs and missing guts, the thing's body is as light as if it were made of paper. Now that Leonidas can see it close up in the light of his torch, he finds it to be closer to human than he would have thought. True, its face is distorted, the skull bulbous in places as though it were a half-cooked pudding or a lopsided dumpling, and its fingers, long and crooked, end in claws, but the anatomy buried at the heart of the thing's misshapen grotesquery is essentially that of a man.

Another trait distinguishes it from the desecrated remains of the Mormon pioneers: its body is as dry as an autumn leaf. Leonidas stuffs great double-handfuls of dry grass beneath the edges of the thing's body and, experimenting, touches his torch to the kindling. The creature burns like its body had been made of oil-soaked wood. The thick black smoke that billows off of its burning carcass is so foul that it makes Leonidas and Miles gag until they move upwind to where Abner reclines atop his coat. The three Pyburns watch in silence as the thing burns. When its bones, which prove drier even than its flesh, burn to glowing chunks, Miles scatters the cinders with his boots, kicking clouds of sparks that flash brilliantly like fireflies in the darkness.

By the time the Pyburns make their way back to camp, weary and filthy, dawn has burnished the Eastern sky. "Hmmm. I suppose you want to rest, Miles?"

"You suppose incorrectly." The defiance has been beaten out of him by the preceding night; his voice is hollow. "I don't think I can rest. We must try to press on. I want a continent between us and this godforsaken place." Abner offers no argument. Moving with limbs that feel like they're shrouded in lead, Leonidas and Miles strike camp and load their meager gear onto the horses. Within an hour of sunrise, they are again mounted and headed west. They move as though in a dream and chase the night shadows as the sun climbs the sky behind them.

¤

It soon becomes obvious that something is amiss with Abner. Leonidas and Miles are exhausted, having spent the hours before dawn wielding shovels, but Abner can barely stay upright in his saddle. He slumps, muttering nonsense and soaked in sweat, until Leonidas calls a halt to their travel, despite the fact that it's not even midday yet. He presses the back of one hand to Abner's forehead and pulls it away quickly. Abner is so engulfed in fever that his skin is practically scalding. By sunset, Abner has lapsed into unconsciousness. He tosses and turns, clothing soaked through with sweat. Every so often, his half-doze is broken by moans of pain. It isn't as simple as the damage done by the bite, although it has taken on a red, inflamed look that Leonidas doesn't like, and the scabbed-over tooth marks have turned black and begun to emanate a fruity, lively stench. No, as near as Leonidas can make out, the primary source of Abner's discomfort is his bones, which feel— he moans, half-conscious— as though they are all burning with brittle fire.

The night is so quiet that even the insects seem to be holding off their usual evening orchestrations. At first, Leonidas— lying awake with his eyes full of frozen starlight— thinks he is imagining the sound. After a few moments, he rolls over in his bedroll and props his head aloft on one arm. He listens carefully, cranes his neck nearer to Abner, and hears the sound again, clear and undeniable in the silence. To Leonidas' fear and horror, Abner's *bones* are *creaking*. They send forth a muted sound like green branches smothered by snow. They moan along with Abner (in their own quiet, calcified way) as they twist and lengthen. By morning, a full four inches of misshapen shin protrude from each pant leg, which, as recently as the previous day, had fit Abner exactly.

By morning, there's no way to deny (nor any point in so doing) that some malign change is being worked in Abner, a painful byproduct (Leonidas can only guess) of the bite given him by the twisted thing in the graveyard. Abner has begun to lose his hair in great double handfuls, and his breathing has become harsh, dry, and ragged. Miles cannot convince

Abner to drink water, not even in the scant moments when his younger brother regains his faculties for a few moments.

Leonidas, numb, watches as the sun rises in its inevitable majesty to officiate another day. It splashes its cold white radiance across a sprawling blue sky. Another day on the flat, featureless grasses of the open territory. By midday, Abner can no longer tolerate the sunlight, which stings his skin and burns his eyes. His discomfort is so profound that before long, he has to take delirious refuge inside his bedroll, and Leonidas and Miles have to rig a halfhearted travois in order to drag him into the shade of a nearby cliff. It's a stubby thing that provides a paltry puddle of shade, but it is enough, for the moment, to relieve Abner's agonies. Miles and Leonidas leave him there, dozing uneasily, as they hobble the horses, make camp, and discuss what has become obvious.

"He's dying," Miles says. There's a desperate edge to his voice that Leonidas hasn't heard before and doesn't like. "He's dying, and I'll be *goddamned* if I'm going to let that happen. I'll ride ahead. I'll find someone who can help, and I'll bring them back."

"I have no doubt that you'd fly with haste. But I doubt that you'd find anyone this far into the territories, let alone someone who could help. And if his condition worsens, I will need you here with me to help care for him."

Although he is the picture of health in comparison to his brother, Miles looks like death warmed over, Leonidas decides, and he tells his oldest son to sleep, even as Abner sleeps. "We'll see how far we can get tonight, when the light won't burn him. Go sleep. I'll take first watch." They are the first kind words he has given Miles since the night of the sexton's fateful intrusion upon their camp, but they seem to roll off of Miles unnoticed. He does take the opportunity to huddle into his bedroll, miserable and limp-looking. Before he can draw two breaths, he is asleep, and Leonidas is alone with his thoughts.

They are grim, Leonidas' thoughts, and they chase each other around his sleep-deprived mind like starving rats. He thinks of the Mormon Swede and his partially-devoured bride, of the thing they had found in the dark, feasting on the dead. Of its slack, almost-human face and warped, twisted limbs. Before long, any thought of sleep has evaporated. Leonidas contents himself with gnawing on some hardtack and sipping water. As sunset fills the Western sky with boiling blood, Leonidas wakes Miles, and the two break camp as quickly as they can. Leonidas' hopes that Abner would be well enough to ride are dashed in short order. He looks sicker than ever. Miles loads him back onto the travois, and the Pyburns resume their travels by the light of the moon, which is cold and clear and causes Abner no evident pain.

The trio crest a hill whose gentle breast stands out on the featureless grass plains. It is the solitary geographic feature, and though its slope is not steep, the way up is slow. As they climb, the moon is obscured by clouds which swamp the open plain in darkness. Leonidas leads the way and crosses the summit of the hill; as he does so, the moon emerges again. As though by divine stagecraft, the plain before them is lit brilliantly. Just ahead, tucked where it had been kept from sight by the hill, was a tiny settlement of boxy wooden structures. They can see a crude church, complete with large Orthodox cross, some houses, and what could perhaps be a general store. Miles perks up immediately at the evidence of human habitation. He unhooks the travois, leaves Abner atop the hill with Leonidas, and rides at a rapid trot down the hill and into the midst of the buildings.

Leonidas could have saved him the trouble. He has been in enough towns and cities to feel, almost instinctually, the presence of other human beings, even those who would no doubt be asleep this deep into the night. Miles checks thoroughly nonetheless, and soon rides back up the hill, dejection showing in every line of his body, from his bowed head to his slumped shoulders and death grip upon the reins of his horse. "Abandoned," is all he says before he tends again to the travois and his sweating, moaning brother.

The chance to sleep inside of a structure beneath a proper roof is too good to pass up, especially with clouds moving in thick on a cold, steady breeze that already carries the first spits of rain. Leonidas notes the meticulous planning that must have gone into the arrangement of everything they pass; the graveyard, tucked away behind the tiny church, is even laid out in neat rows, each grave marked by a sun-bleached wooden Orthodox cross. Their shelter for the night is to be an abandoned house, not far from the church. Once Abner is tucked away inside, muttering and moaning in his bedroll, Miles returns to the picket fence that surrounds the church. Leonidas hears the ferocious cracking of the wooden joints there as Miles kicks them to pieces with his boots. He returns to the house a few moments later, red-faced and sweating, but calmer, and bearing in his arms a great load of dry wood. Soon, a fire burns in the house's stone hearth, and though the room around them is devoid of furniture, it feels almost like a home as they sit on the floor by the fire. Leonidas makes sure that Abner is far enough from the flames to be safe, and before long, even though no watch has been set, Leonidas drowns in sleep.

When he wakes, the silence is eerie in its depth. The rain has stopped, and the cold air is perfumed with its passage. The fire has died down to a fitful carpet of glowing coals. Miles, still deep, deep in sleep, is a dark, silent lump in his bedroll. It takes Leonidas a moment to remember where he is, and another moment still to determine what's wrong with the scene before him: he can no longer hear Abner's moans. In fact, Abner's clothing and bedroll are wadded up like a snake's shed skin in the corner. Abner himself is nowhere to be seen. Leonidas feels a sickened ripple run through his guts like melting ice. The mud— and the moonlight that glimmers on its surface like a scattering of pale gems— makes Abner easy to track. It would, in fact, be hard to miss his tracks; they are the only ones visible, and his bare feet have left long, strange-looking impressions on its surface that lead in a line as inevitable and fatal as the pull of gravity. They lead to the little graveyard behind the chapel, the one marked by the Orthodox wooden crosses.

Abner is there, naked and as pale-white as a grub writhing beneath an upturned rock— though his legs to the knee and his arms to the elbow are painted in mud. He has unearthed a corpse from its shallow grave beneath the symbol of the crucifixion, of death and rebirth.

As Leonidas watches, Abner plucks a dainty from deep within the bowels of the corpse and, lifting it to his spattered face, begins to eat.

Chapter Four

It's more than Leonidas can bear to watch for more than a few moments. They are moments that will forever be seared into his mind's eye, waiting for quiet hours in which to creep up on him and whisper in his ear. The convulsive bobbing of Abner's long, misshapen throat, the new shape of his skull, and, most of all, the guttural noises of sensual pleasure that escape his lips…these things strike at Leonidas in a place far deeper than he would have suspected existed inside of him. Without thinking, his hand steals to his pocket, the heavy lump of gold there on its fine golden chain. He squeezes it and feels tiny chips of gemstone dig into his palm and bite him in a way that brings sweet pinpoints of pain.

He picks his way back to the house where Miles still sleeps, careful to tread as lightly as he can. He needn't have bothered; Abner, naked and gleaming in the moonlight, is absorbed in his midnight feast. He doesn't seem to notice Leonidas at all. The elder Pyburn's guts are a boiling kettle of snakes as he sits near the dying fire and waits for Abner to return to bed. Dawn arrives, filling the sky with turquoise and peaches; there is still no sign of him. Leonidas wakes Miles, and although he spares him any description of his brother's hideous meal, he says enough to convey, in broad strokes, that something terrible has been wrought in Abner. Miles, for his part, is quieter by far than Leonidas has ever seen him, and accepts what his father says without challenge or argument.

The one emotion that Miles gives voice to is worry. "You saw what the sun was doing to him? He can't be out there now; he'll burn to death." Leonidas can't argue with that, and the two set off in the direction of the graveyard. Abner has been busy. The desecration of a handful of graves and the half-eaten state of the rotting corpses that have been left, strewn about the ground, are testimony to his industriousness. If Leonidas sought to spare Miles the knowledge of what his brother had been up to, the remains of his handiwork dispel those hopes immediately. It is, in a word, obvious what Abner has done. Miles is pale, his brow dappled with clammy sweat, but he stays by his father's side, unflinching. The aftermath of his night in the graveyard, however, is the only sign of Abner that they see. He is nowhere to be found in the cemetery. The pastel light of dawn washes over the ghost town; during the night, more rain had done the same, erasing Abner's footprints.

They find him a short time later. Leonidas and Miles are certain that Abner would have taken refuge from the day's sunrise, and they search the little ghost-settlement one building at a time. The place is an eerie sight. The windows in some houses still bear partial panes of glass, but all the furnishings are absent. Tall grass has begun to twine itself through some of the floorboards; stalks lift their heavy, bearded seedpods in the stillness of the abandoned rooms like penitents in Nature's cathedral. Abner is in the root cellar of an empty house not far from the one in which they'd spent the night, as it turns out. He huddles in one corner of the cellar's earthen floor, naked and insensate, his arms and legs caked in filth whose provenance Leonidas chooses not to think about too deeply. Abner, Leonidas figures, must have been drawn to the root cellar by the damp darkness, by the shelter it offers from the sun. They leave Abner there, slumbering in filthy darkness, and debate the matter back at the empty house in which they'd taken shelter the night before.

"We cannot travel all the way to California by cover of darkness, Miles. And supposing we did, what then? Do you think a doctor can help him now? How long do you think he has, out on the trail, up in the Rockies?"

"So, we *leave* him here? To what *end*? What do you think he will do here— how long will he last? Merciful *Christ*, father!"

What Leonidas does *not* say is: "His supply of food, as horrible as it is to think about, will hold out as long as that little graveyard does." What Leonidas says, instead, is: "He has shelter here. We are far enough from Crow country that he will likely be unmolested. He'd be close to a stream, to fresh water. If you think you can find a doctor who can help him, by all means, we shall return here posthaste." Leonidas is astonished at how confident he sounds saying these things, how easy it is to lie to Miles. *Maybe,* he thinks, *the Leonidas of the West is one who has no qualms about dissembling. What other talents wait to be discovered out here in this erasure?*

Miles, for his part, is willing to be convinced, though his shoulders sag and his eyes are downcast when he agrees to leave Abner in the root cellar. Miles packs Abner's gear onto his horse, and, while he does, Leonidas does his best to reassemble the graves uprooted by Abner. He is driven by the ghost of a compulsion to neatness. He feels like a fool doing this, given that they're leaving Abner here to repeat the vandalism (*and necrophagy,* Leonidas thinks before he can stop himself) of the preceding evening. When the bodies are half-buried in shallow dirt, he catches himself short and utters an oath as he flings the shovel away from him. Why bother, when he knows what will inevitably happen, when, in fact, he is relying on these rotting, half-desiccated corpses to provide for his ruined son?

Leonidas wanders through the tiny cemetery in the direction he threw his shovel. He trails his fingers along the wooden markers, stopping every so often to read one— or try to, at any rate. Among the curling Cyrillic of the names and short epitaphs, the dates are about the only thing he can make out. Using them, Leonidas pieces together that illness or another calamity had killed a great many of the ghost town's residents the preceding year. In Nauvoo, Leonidas had heard of religious dissenters and splinter faiths that had fled the Russian Empire in search of religious and political freedom in the open West. The tiny, abandoned town had been some community's attempt to realize their Kingdom of Heaven. It had failed, wrecked on the rocks of disease or famine or some other misfortune out here, far from assistance or aid. *Do people*, Leonidas wonders, *ever tire of trying to create Heaven on Earth? Do they never learn what such attempts actually bring to Earth, the Hell they make of life?* Leonidas thinks of Christiansen, the Mormon cemetery in Winter Quarters, and the hundreds of dead buried there, and supposes that he has his answer already. He just doesn't like what the answer is.

By the time that Leonidas wanders back to Miles, camp has been struck, the horses loaded, and Abner's mount tied on a lead. Miles slumps in the saddle, his shoulders tense and the set of his face miserable. He has his back to the house in whose cellar Abner slumbers on, changed and changing still. He spares not so much as a glance back at the ghost settlement where they leave his brother. Leonidas can tell that of the pain that they've endured since the sexton had wandered out of the night with his mangled hand, this is the most acute, this abandonment of Abner to the little ghost town and the banquet rotting beneath its churchyard.

Miles' silence continues unabated as they ride. The cerulean dawn gives way to a grey morning and an even greyer day. The thunderclouds are as heavy and swollen overhead as great black lakes suspended in the sky, but the rain holds back. The chill air is pregnant with it, and as Leonidas and Miles leave the small rise beyond the ghost town, the sky dances with brilliant blue-white lightning, and thunder rolls across the featureless grass plain in rippling sheets of sound that boom and echo like the wrath of some pagan god— a God of Thunder, perhaps. Eventually, the rain *does* come, tired of toying with the arid grass of the plains. It arrives in sheets so thick and cold that it's like a baptism— *or*, Leonidas thinks, *a drowning*. The two Pyburn men ride in miserable, rain-soaked silence. Even the horses hang their heads and snort their displeasure, their sodden manes hanging in ropes almost to the mud beneath their hooves.

After a long, bone-chilling hour, they ride to a small cliff face whose concave surface provides shelter from the down-pour. There they make camp, unsure of the precise moment when the feeble light of day ends and the gloom of the rainy evening becomes the black, thunder-riddled dark of night. The rain goes on and on, and as Miles and Leonidas hunker beside their meager cook-fire, they say nothing. Leonidas glances at Miles from time to time. He doesn't care for the va-cancy in those eyes, the darkness that seems imported from the night's stormy sky overhead and into his gaze: abyss, flashes of lightning and all. For the first time since they began their trek to California those months before, Leonidas wonders if there is violence in his elder son, if he should, in fact, be afraid of Miles on some level. *The young devour the old*, thinks Leonidas, *and why not? That's the natural order of things.* The fate that had befallen Abner back at Winter Quarters— *that* was unnatural. And this brooding lout of a son had had a hand in that bloody nonsense, his cowardice expensive beyond an ordinary reckoning. *The young eat the old, is that it? Well, we will see about that. I have fangs enough to fend for myself.* It doesn't take Leonidas long to talk himself from fear into anger, and the two men pass the night in a sullen funk.

The next day brings sunlight, sweet and warm, and the sound of ecstatic birdsong before the dawn, a chorus that builds to a loud cacophony by the time that they resume their travels. Leonidas, his mood of the preceding night lifted somewhat by the beautiful day, calls back, "We should make South Pass by evening. We're making good time, Miles, hmmm?" Miles does not answer, although his silence now seems more contemplative than despondent. *Something* is obviously weighing on his mind, thoughts that he chews over silently, and as joylessly as he gnaws on his midday meal of jerky and hardtack.

The ground begins to rise beneath their feet, sloping gently upwards as they approach the Pass. This is, Leonidas knows, a new route, and one that is far, far more forgiving than the mountains that previous parties had hacked their way through. South Pass, he suspects, will become a way-point for those headed West— the obvious choice for wagon trains, yes, but no less preferable for a party as small as theirs. They crest the last rise, and there they are, atop the Continental Divide, looking past the Rocky Mountains and at an endless brown horizon of low, grassy, sloping land, the bottom of which gleams with the silver ribbon of a small river. It's a beautiful sight, the sight both of a limitless expanse of easily traversable land and for what it implies: the beginning of the conclusion of their journey, progress within sight— and therefore within reach. Leonidas almost feels light as they make camp that night, and he whistles a bit to himself as he cooks a pot of beans laced with salt-cured bacon, a rare feast drawn from their limited stock of supplies. Miles picks joylessly at his plate until Leonidas, thoroughly disgusted by his failure to see the positive side of the day's travel, snatches it from his hands and finishes it himself.

When Miles speaks up, his voice startles Leonidas badly: at first because of its clarity in the silence of the evening, and then because of *what* he says.

"I do not think," Miles says, "that I will go to California with you, father. In fact, I know I will not. I have no place there without Abner. I have no place *anywhere* that I can think of, but I have an idea of where to start. I'll be parting ways with you here. I'm going to follow the Saints' wagon trains and see where their prophet's legacy takes them. I think I owe it to Christiansen to find his people, if he has any, and tell them that he is buried with his wife. I think, too, that what you said— about death— it can't be true. Death and darkness and, what was it you said, dissolution?"

"Miles, this is absurd. You cannot do this. We have a place in California— we have a destiny there. What happened to Abner is horrible: put it out of your mind." Leonidas hesitates, then continues. "Not all of us can be brave, son, and there's no more shame in that than there is in anything else, I suppose."

"Oh?" asks Miles. "Yes, maybe. But maybe I can....progress? What was it you said the Saints believe in— eternal progression?"

"It is a child's fantasy, Miles." Leonidas can scarcely credit what he is hearing. He had expected *something* dramatic from Miles, a reaction to match his gutlessness and hand-wringing over Abner, but never in his wildest nightmares had he imagined something like this: a religious awakening. *Are both of my sons ruined, then*? He thinks. *It's almost enough to make one believe in a deity, if only to have someone to hate.*

"Maybe." Miles sounds as though he has genuinely considered this possibility. "But I like the odds better with the Saints than I do with you, father." With that, the matter appears closed, and Miles will brook no more debate on the subject.

As it turns out, Miles has been hiding his skill as a navigator and reader of maps. It doesn't take him long to pick out the route known to be favored by the Latter Day Saints and to chart a brief detour that will put him along the path of their wagon trains within a few days. "A group led by the Donners cleared a forest pass to the North, and I should be able to find ample sign of their wagons without much trouble. The Donners cut their way through with wagons, which the Saints have, as well. It should be easy enough for a single man on horseback to follow. I've been thinking this through, father. There is nothing waiting in California for me, not without Abner." Leonidas, his heart now growing heavy with the knowledge that Miles means to follow through on his absurd plan, tries one more time.

"Do not do this, Miles. What makes you think you will be welcome wherever their portable madhouse fetches up?"

Miles smiles, and there is depthless sadness in it. "I expect I *won't* be welcome. At first. But eternal progression— I like what that implies about my chances of being welcome. At some point. Perhaps even before I die." Leonidas has nothing to say to that and attempts no reply.

That night, Leonidas dreams. In his dream, he, Miles,

and Abner are lost in a cavern, a massive underground gallery of weird mineral traces that shine in a directionless light with no apparent source. The vaulted ceiling, high overhead, echoes with the hard sound of their horses' hooves as they pick their way through the damp stone. Leonidas leads his sons, and he is desperate for them not to know how lost he is, how frightened, how he has no memory of sunlight nor of how they managed to wind up in this terrible predicament, turned around and rudderless in the endless stone intestines of the caves.

Leonidas and the Pyburn brothers round an especially strange-looking rock formation, a twisted thing like a great, leering face, and are greeted by a broad, black, silent river that flows sluggishly around the teeth of the stalagmites and down the gullet of the caves to God alone knows where. Its oily surface and opaque depths fill Leonidas with an unreasoning terror, but he — he *must* not, he tells himself—show his sons how frightened he is.

"We'll ford it," Abner says brightly, and Leonidas feels his guts turn to jelly at the thought.

"You'll be lost," comes Miles' voice from behind Leonidas, and there is great, boundless sorrow in it. "We'll all be lost and never found again. Down in the dark. Down at the bottom of the river of the dead. We are trespassers who have carried our hunger into hungry country."

Abner swings out of his saddle and, taking his horse's reins in his hand, plunges into the river without so much as a backward glance. "*Abner!*" Leonidas screams. He dismounts his horse with clumsy, panicked haste and plunges into the river after Abner. His fear of the river is forgotten; the only thing he can feel is a terrible, numbing certainty that this scene will play itself out as it has before, as it must always do. And, sure enough, he can do little else but watch as Abner sinks beneath the oily water. His head emerges once; his eyes roll with terror, and foaming water falls from his mouth as he drowns. Leonidas plunges his arms into the water desperately, again and again, reaching for Abner but falling short with every attempt. And the water is cold, so cold. It sucks the strength from his arms, and, before long, his legs buckle under him, and he is himself swallowed by the dark, by the freezing blackness of the silent river. His last sight before he sinks beneath the tumult of the waters completely is of Miles, watching from the shore with eyes that shine like secret silver, like dead coins flashing their cold brilliance in the shadows of this cave, the Plutonian labyrinth where Leonidas will die, just as Abner died.

Leonidas wakes with a drowning man's gasp of mortal terror. For a split second, he can taste the black, stony water of the cavern again, filling his gullet, but when he turns and retches as though to clear his lungs of water, nothing emerges from his mouth but a long rope of drool. He sits up in the dark, gasping for breath, trying to regain his composure. By the time he falls asleep once more, the dream's strange power over his thoughts has lifted.

In the morning, the two men part ways without embracing. Each goes his own direction with his own thoughts, bathed in sunlight and the song of innumerable birds, a riotous sound of life in a place that has shown them so much death.

Interlude: 1855

Whack… whack… whack…

Each time that the heavy wooden door of the cabin bangs shut in the moaning wind, Turner flinches. His movements are severely restricted, folded as he is into his hiding place behind Bonhoeffer's cot, and a few times his jerking start at the sound cracks his head painfully against the cot's wooden frame. His great, bulbous eyes stare wildly and bulge from his sweating skull even more than they usually do. He has developed a tic at the corner of one of them, and it pulls an entire quadrant of his face into twitching disarray. His body trembles and shakes within the sweaty and unwashed shell

83

of his clothes, and his skin has attained such a greasy pallor, all the way up to the bald crown of his head, that he resembles nothing so much as a shivering wax figurine. Turner, in short, has reached the end of his rope and dangles there, engulfed by fear.

How long have they been here now, up the creeks and waterways from Lake Superior, untold miles deep into the virgin timber they'd come to cut? Months. Longer, in fact, than the contract out of Thunder Bay, Ontario had specified—longer by weeks. Hadn't that been why they'd been caught out here by the snowstorm? It had blown in from Superior, an invading army of iron thunderheads which had, in short order, begun to shroud their campsite in snow. After one day of the blizzard, it became clear they wouldn't be able to strike camp until its wrath abated. After two days, the men had moved their bedrolls from their canvas tents—which had begun to sag and collapse under the onslaught—to the site's single permanent structure, a one-room log cabin of crude but sturdy construction. It had been built by French furriers nearly a half-century gone from the area and eagerly adopted by the timber-men who'd followed.

Whack… WHACK!

The door, caught by a well-timed gust of wind, slams shut with more force than usual before banging open again. Turner— twitching, miserable— jerks convulsively at the sound and yelps. He is immediately furious with himself and redoubles his internal debate: ignore the door or creep carefully forth to securely close it? *If I stay low to the floor*, he thinks, *as low as a snake, it won't be able to see me, not through the cabin's one tiny window, not in this storm.*

Will it?

He mops sweat from his narrow, mournful features and listens to his heart as it hammers in his chest, almost in time to the damnable flapping of the cabin's door.

Whack… whack… whack…

After three days of snow, three days of unending frozen darkness, they'd heard something. A man shouting, by the sound of it, raving and raging in a dialect that one of the men thinks he recognizes as Algonquian. Turner, as the camp's cook and its part-time barber and surgeon, sat low on the pecking order established early on by the men; as a result, it was his lot to be squeezed into a space near the window, where there was a persistent and troublesome draft. A draft, but also a view of the little clearing outside the cabin with its sad circle of half-collapsed tents. So it was that he was the first of the camp's men to actually lay eyes on the thing as it stumbled out of the trees.

"Blessed *Virgin*," Turner had exclaimed from his perch near the crack in the shutters. "Some moon-eyed idiot is out there afoot— and *bare-chested*, if you can believe it!"

"Chippewa?" That had been DuPont, and his hands had tightened on the stock of his rifle as he'd asked the question.

"Could be. Damned hard to see *anything*."

The voice that had continued to float out of the snow was clear and insistent, shouting its incomprehensible message in Algonquian. Faucheux, the sole member of their party with any proficiency in Indian languages, had only been able to pick out a few words, and they'd sounded like nonsense. Then, as the curtain of falling snow had parted for just a moment, Turner got a good look at the intruder. (*Is* he *the intrud-*

er? Turner's treasonous back-mind had whispered. *Aren't* we *the intruders?*) Chippewa, maybe, to judge by the long black hair, straight as a midnight waterfall, and, yes, bare from the waist up, and so covered in flecks and flakes of snow that he might have been made entirely of the stuff, were he not ambulating forth from the trees with slow, trudging steps.

Faucheux, who had the softest heart of the party when it came to the native denizens of Superior's shores, had got one look at the man through Turner's window and had started immediately for the front door. The door, heavy as it was, had to be tied closed from the inside against the wind, and Faucheux had set to untying it. Against the exhortations of the other men in the cabin, out he had gone, intending to save the poor, snow-tossed madman.

"Do you need help?" Faucheux's voice could hardly be heard above the wind. Each word had produced a plume of steaming breath from his lips that the storm snatched greedily away. "*Pouvons-nous vous aider?*"

The stranger had certainly *looked* like he needed help. Though there was no visible injury on his person, the interloper's ragged trousers were stained red-to-black with what was unmistakably blood. The stranger's head had whipped around, fixing on Faucheux's location as he had answered in that same clear, ringing voice: "*Oui! Je suis perdu!*" Yes! I am lost! Faucheux had reached the man's side and swung an arm over his naked shoulders with the intent of steering him toward the warmth and shelter of the cabin. As Faucheux had engaged in this act of heroic charity, two realizations had fallen on Turner like lead weights. The first was that this visitor to their campsite was naked to the waist. The snowflakes should have melted against the heat of his skin, coating him in droplets. Instead, they landed and accumulated as though his flesh were as chilly as ice. Second, though the voice that answered Faucheux's query was clear as a bell, it was not accompanied by a plume of steam: the stranger's breath, like his body, was, by all appearances, as cold and as lifeless as the snow-choked sky.

Before Turner could fully articulate any of this— let alone shout a warning of some kind to Faucheux—a particularly vicious squall of wind had picked up and carried a curtain of snow through the clearing, obscuring his view. When it had cleared, moments later, Faucheux and the stranger were gone.

Perhaps satiated by the toll already exacted from the men, the storm had partially withdrawn its wrath overnight. By dawn of the fourth day, the sun's light had been anemic, but visible, and the wind and snow had lessened from a roar to a mutter. Three of the men— DuPont, Schroeder, and Black— had armed themselves as best they could (DuPont's rifle being the camp's only firearm in working order) and left in search of Faucheux, who had been well-liked. Faucheux, regrettably, was not to be seen again. Nor were Schroeder and Black. DuPont returned well after dark that night, terrified and raving about a devil-possessed Chippewa who addressed him in the idiomatic French of the long-lost Montreal slum where DuPont had been born. Strong as a team of oxen, it had spirited him away as easily as a grown man might carry an infant and only revealed its true face when Schroeder and Black had, in pursuing him, taken the bait. It was not a face he felt prepared to describe, nor would Turner press him on the matter. Whatever had taken place out in the moaning snow, in the frozen woods, had coated his clothing in a good amount of mysterious blood. It had also driven him quite insane. He'd scarcely been back an hour when he struggled free and plunged into the night once more, screaming that they'd all die, that he'd rather die making a go for Thunder Bay. The darkness had swallowed him like a gnat.

That left just Turner and Ransom in the cabin, two miserable men huddled by the dying heat of the stove (dying, cruel as it was, for neither one of them cared to venture out for more wood). It had been the two of them, at any rate, until Ransom had let his guard down near the window, where he'd been checking and rechecking the tree-line. Before Turner was fully aware of what was transpiring (indeed, before even Ransom seemed to have an idea), a long, bloodsoaked arm snaked through the crack in the shutters. The poor woodsman was hauled, screaming, through the wreckage of the shutters and out into the storm. This time, perhaps spurred by fear of being left alone with the murderous Chippewa, Turner had burst from the cabin's door in an attempt to save Ransom.

He had not saved Ransom. As he'd rounded the corner of the cabin, he was greeted by the sight of the big Indian, shirtless— but ice-cold no more. Instead, he was clad in a mantle of Ransom's tacky, rapidly-freezing blood, which smoked and steamed in the cold air as the thing (he could no longer consider it a man) methodically disassembled Ransom's screaming body. It was a sight from Hell itself, and Turner had crept back inside without so much as a peep.

Did it see me? The thought pounds, now, as desperately as his heart. *Did it see me? Did it see me?*

Whack. …. WHACK.

How long has he crouched beside the stove? Five minutes? An hour? *"Screw yer suet-guts to yer worthless spine!"* The voice that shifts Turner into motion may be inside his head, but it is as clear as if his father— five years dead— were in the room barking directly into his ear. *"Get, boy! Get!"* Ever the obedient son, Turner shuffles forward, as low to the ground as he can bend his screaming spine, and makes it past the stove… Past the window… And to the door. He braces his shoulder against it and leans, hard, into the wind, slowly pushing it closed.

At the last moment, there is an explosive impact against the door that brings it up hard against Turner's face, splitting his lip. He falls back and lands on his ass with a breathtaking impact. The door slams back against its frame as if it weighs nothing at all, and the spare winter light is blotted out by a silhouette. Turner recoils in terror, but only for a moment. It is not the shirtless, murder-drunk Chippewa he sees. No, instead, he is greeted by the sight of an Indian woman, clad from boots to flop-brimmed hat in motley leathers. Little more than her flashing eyes are visible between the layers wrapped around her against the storm, but the curves of her hips and breasts reveal her gender even if the ferocity of her gaze does not. Her appraisal of him is brutal, silent, and takes scant moments: this quivering jelly of a man before her is not her quarry, not the spirit she has followed to this place all the way from the land that has exiled her.

Before she can finish, the pointed steel end of the peavey— the long lumber-hook— rips through her mouth from the cheek inwards, curtailing her remarks. Her startled eyes, rocked by the impact of the tool's metal against her skull, lose their focus. She chokes once, sending a tiny spurt of blood from beneath her bandana, and then sags and tumbles down the cabin's crooked steps. Her form in the doorway is replaced by that of the big man, the thing that the woman had referred to as the Wolf's Mouth. He is as broad as the doorway, and this close to him in the flesh, a few things become obvious.

First of all, the Mouth, despite his ease in ambulation, is quite dead. He is also filled with madness, if it is possible for the dead to be mad— perhaps for the dead to *go* mad. It dances in his guttering eyes and radiates from his flesh in freezing waves. The Mouth's eyes glow with a dull, mossy luminescence that lights them in their sockets despite the deep shadows of the cabin's doorway. Turner can't look away; it's like being hypnotized by two small, infected suns. He feels truly helpless. His is the terror of the rat cornered by the serpent, or the vole swept up by the silent knives of the owl's talons.

"Hi-*ho*!" it booms. "What a *harvest* have we, yes we *do*!" Long, gore-blackened fingers grip the doorjamb with a rotten creak. The thing festering inside the big Chippewa man tenses its arms, its limber legs, and leaps in one bound from the doorway to the floor before Turner. The Mouth lands with a heavy, meaty thud that Turner can feel through his tailbone as he scrambles backward, terrified.

"Oh, there'll be *no* interrupting bitches this day, no, *sir*!" it thunders. Its breath is awful, all corroded copper and dripping meat, and Turner is filled with the terrible certainty that it has been eating of the dead outside: feasting upon the hunks and chunks left by its terrible wrath. "Just *sport*! Sport and *play*, yes, *sirrah*!" Its grin is so wide that the hinges of its skull creak. Whatever thing this is, speaking to him through this big man's corpse, it isn't human— was *never* human; this much is clear from its horrible bog-light eyes. Turner has seen mayhem done in drunken passion before, a few times. Once, he'd even seen a man lose a hand to a terrible knife wound. He'd seen the light of murder in the eyes of the man wielding the blade that night; this is nothing like that. This is something as alien to humanity as to reason. *This will be a bad death*, he thinks.

"Hey!" comes a voice from behind it. The Mouth turns, and Turner scrambles past one of its legs in a mad dash for safety. He is, for the moment, forgotten as the thing whirls to face the person addressing it. It's the Indian woman. In one hand, she wields a long-handled wood axe. Somehow— he has no idea how— she has worked the peavey out of her face. The metal hook left a gaping wound in her cheek through which Turner can see white teeth and the gleam of gums. Blood flows freely from the wounds in her cheek and up her lips, framing a great, wet, crimson grin, a hot expression of genuine joy. *That*, he decides, *is the face of a warrior*. At the same moment, he is filled with a deep certainty that he has no further interest in war, had he any to begin with.

¤

Left Hand cannot feel her face, but she had felt meat part from bone when she'd pulled the hook from her mouth. Her vision is blurred and shifts in and out of focus. These concerns are far from Left Hand's mind; she is ecstatic.

95

The Mouth bellows at her— a deep, distorted, discordant sound more like the groan of a gored bull than a sound made by a human. It plants its feet, tenses, and leaps again, this time at Left Hand. She is ready. She swings the axe with a natural grace and economy of movement that would have been almost like a dance in other circumstances. In these circumstances, her balletic efforts serve her well. The sharp curve of the axe blade hits her adversary square in the face just below the nose. The stroke has such momentum behind it that the impact neatly bisects the head of the body bearing the Wolf's Mouth. The top of the skull— twitching eyes and all—sails lazily through the air and lands with a *thwap*. The thing's arms and legs go rigid, and it crashes to the wooden floor of the cabin next to Left Hand. Blood drains from the rim of its truncated skull in freshets. Its lips, Turner sees, still twist and sneer convulsively. It is only when the lips have stilled— when the fingers no longer clutch and spasm— that Left Hand takes her eyes off of it and tends to the deep wounds in her face. It is this task she is engaged in, pressing a wad of burlap to her bleeding face, when Turner approaches her.

"What…was it? Where did it come from?" He hesitates. "Are there… more of them?"

"An intruder. Somewhere else." She regards the dull gleam of the axe's silver head through its rime of blood, the handle, straight and sturdy. She plucks it from the ground and slides it into the belt of her leathers, where it rests as though designed just for her. "And I certainly hope so. As it turns out, there is plenty of gold in killing monsters."

She sags to a seat near the door. The wound in her face has already soaked through its makeshift burlap bandage.

"Gold and monsters; they always find each other." And with that, Left Hand loses consciousness.

¤

She will not regain her senses until three days later when the storm has cleared. Turner tends her as best he can throughout these days; he even manages to feed her a little broth and water, boiled at the stove that once again— with the threat outside removed— can be fed. Throughout this, Left Hand raves and mutters. Some of the things that Turner overhears are beautiful. Some are terrible. He will repeat nary a word of it for the rest of his days but will treasure the words she spilled— his own secret knowledge of a great mystery. At length, her head clears, and though her fever still smolders, her strength returns. "There is something in the West," is all she will tell him about her plans. "An unfinished thing that needs to be finished."

Weeks after the coming of the snow, Turner and Left Hand make their way out of the cabin, slowly down the streams, and to a timber camp on the shore of Lake Superior.

Part II: 1870

Chapter Five

The train pulls into the station, a modest little building for a place growing as fast as Great Salt Lake City. Leonidas dismounts the car slowly, his joints stiff from the long train ride. When he sighs, he can taste the fresh-cut wood of the station on his tongue as he inhales. It's good to taste city air again, redolent of cinders and horse excrement and commerce. He feels expansive, relieved to be released after his confinement aboard the train. Luxury box or no (and the accommodations had been, he has to admit, more suitable than he had feared they might be), it had been a long trip from San Francisco, and Leonidas is not as spry as he'd been as a middle-aged man, let alone a young one. Nor was he any longer accustomed to crowds. *There was a time*, he reflects, *in '50 or '55, perhaps, when I would have relished this crush of humanity, knowing as I do my station compared to theirs. The company of my fellow man has lost its novelty.*

His ebony cane's gold tip, accented with elaborate filigree, taps against the steps as he descends to the platform. He slips one hand into a vest pocket and retrieves a small pocket watch— also gold— and checks the time. "Hmmm." He stands clear of the steps, executing a half-turn that's almost nimble, and watches as an enormous man emerges from the luxury box. He cuts quite the figure: broad-chested, broad-faced, and sporting a pair of curly, bright red mutton-chop sideburns. The big man carries Leonidas' luggage, and though the bags are large, heavy leathern things, he bears them as though they are no more than soap bubbles.

Leonidas smooths his frock coat, fusses for a moment with the gold stick-pin in his loosely tied tie, and watches the big man set his bags carefully to one side. "Mister Brimelow?" Leonidas inquires. His tone is polite, his voice hoarse. "Would you be so good as to see about a coach?"

Brimelow gazes at Leonidas with dull green eyes, low under the brim of his beaten bowler hat, and nods. His shoulders roll easily as he ambles away, arms as large and as hard as two tree trunks. He is poorly contained by his cheap suitcoat. Leonidas, on the other hand, is resplendent in his spotless black frock-coat and starched white shirt, his loud checked trousers, and gold watch-fob. He cuts a dandy figure, but even a crown and purple robes would have been a deceptively modest sartorial choice. He is, after all, one of the richest men ever produced by one of the richest nations in the history of the world. He is also, he is all-too-aware, beginning to look, well... old. His moustache and beard, groomed exquisitely, are as white as frost at dawn, as is his hair, slicked back and, for the most part, hidden beneath his top hat.

Leonidas waits for Brimelow and the carriage near his neatly stacked luggage and gazes at the street before him. It's as broad as a river and busy, peopled by coaches and men on horseback. Tall telegraph poles line the thoroughfare's west side, and the sight of the wire snaking from pole to pole brings Leonidas a bit of reassurance. Great Salt Lake City might be remote, he reminds himself, part of the troubled Utah Territory and populated by men and women (a great many women, he notes, watching the street) with strange beliefs. In the end, it doesn't matter: the railroad has brought new blood and a measure of prosperity to the place, whatever the original inhabitants' opinion of the influx, and the telegraph lines are further evidence that the strange new Mormon appendage of Utah Territory is now well-connected to the nerve cluster of California (and the civilized world east of the Mississippi). On the whole, he feels reassured by his initial impressions. Great Salt Lake City does not reek of danger the way some frontier towns he has visited do, nor does it seem at first glance the hive of esoteric cultists that he had thought more likely.

After perhaps a half-hour, a coach pulls up near the Utah Central Railway Depot, driven by a fellow with a squashed and mournful face. The carriage disgorges Brimelow, whose broad, beefy frame barely fits through its door. He loads the luggage atop the coach, steps to one side as Leonidas climbs inside, then squeezes himself into the coach after his employer. It's a tight fit, and Brimelow smells like a man who has been traveling for days, but it's better, Leonidas reminds himself, than a long walk which would reveal how stiff and painful his joints really are.

"I told the driver that you wanted to visit the boneyard." Brimelow's voice is all gravel and pitch, and it carries just a hint of the Irish about it, although Brimelow obviously has taken pains to Americanize his pronunciation.

"That's good," Leonidas replies and cranes his neck to look out the window of the coach as the horses clip and clop their way along the broad street.

It's a young city. That much is apparent. Innumerable trees, planted by the settlers and Saints, form neat lines that are visible from the street, as are a few finely-crafted homes, two- and three-story structures that wouldn't look out of place in San Francisco or Oakland. *And those*, Leonidas reminds himself, *are thriving port cities and centers of commerce.* While the rush for silver in Utah (and the railroad) is sure to spark feverish growth, Great Salt Lake City is a long way from any of the population centers Leonidas considers "civilized" places. Then again, the war had proven that even "civilized" places were but two or three tiny steps from outright butchery and barbarism— if the war had proven anything.

All of that conflict seems remote from this place, though; its industrious energy and cheer are infectious, its young trees and fine houses signs of burning optimism. Leonidas does not share the sentiment, but values it nonetheless for the texture it adds to life in the West. He has seen places with the hope beaten out of them, and while there were certainly advantages to crushing the love of the future out of a place— he had had to resort to such methods a number of times in the pursuit of his mining operations—it was still pleasurable to look at the rows of saplings and allow himself, even if only for a moment, to imagine a bright future.

The busy avenue he travels is dominated by one enormous structure, visible from the Depot and, as they grow nearer, all the more impressive given the modest state of surrounding development. It looks much like cathedrals that

Leonidas has seen. Thick walls of granite rise into the sky. Stained glass glows, a rainbow of jewel colors. Intricate and exquisite details have been poured into every corner, nook, and cranny of its construction. Not quite yet completed but more solid than the foundation of most American dreams: the Mormon Temple, holiest of holies for their faith.

He has to admit, it's a magnificent sight, even in its partially-finished state. *Cathedrals*, he thinks, *used to be the work of centuries*. What further indication of the progress of American man did he need other than the relatively rapid construction of an edifice this fine? Leonidas has to pay his grudging respects as they travel past it; it is a genuinely beautiful structure. The fulfillment of Mormon planning and Mormon craftsmanship, it speaks highly of them as a people.

The air is warm for April, and in the dying light of the day, the scent of some flower— unfamiliar to Leonidas— fills the air with swirling perfume. The light cast by the setting sun is a warm, buttery yellow, and it provides the spotless granite of which the Temple is constructed a glittering carapace studded with mica starbursts. Everything— the neatly maintained dirt roads, the walls of the Temple, the buildings rising along South Temple Street— all of it glows, enchanted by the magic of the setting sun. In spite of himself, Leonidas feels his heart swell and thinks *it* is *beautiful, this city where Miles has made his home.*

Miles. Leonidas tries not to dwell on the choices made by his eldest son, on Miles' religious conversion or the life of quiet, saintly virtue he had described in the one letter he had sent Leonidas over the preceding decades. *My family*, the letter had stated, *lives in the house I built, near the Salt Lake City Cemetery on Wall Street*. Leonidas, who has been to New York City, found this to be a ridiculous affectation— *Wall Street, indeed*, he had snorted— but as the coach draws near to the edge of the Cemetery, Leonidas is seduced by the small, neat homes with their nascent yards, the scent of flowers, the sweetness of the air against his skin, warm and dry.

He had not answered Miles' letter until a few days ago, and his own missive had been curt: *Miles. Will be there soon— matters to discuss.*

A few minutes later, the coach pulls up at the edge of a

sweeping carpet of green studded with young trees. Grave markers, most of which are made of modest-looking stone, form neat lines that stretch out from the low wall that encloses its border, with empty green space beyond them waiting to be filled in by the dead. In fact, as the coach creaks to a stop at a barked order from Brimelow, a fresh grave is being dug right before their eyes. The work is being performed by a stout fellow clad in stained canvas trousers, a sweat-soaked wool shirt, and leather suspenders. He wields a long-handled shovel with a weary indifference Leonidas knows all too well from his interactions with the laborers in his mines. When the coach stops at the edge of the Cemetery and Leonidas emerges from it, watch-fob and stick-pin shining with the radiance of real gold lit by a perfect spring sunset, the gravedigger stops his work and leans on the handle of his shovel. He watches as Leonidas makes his stiff way through a gap in the Cemetery wall and to the edge of the half-dug grave.

"You look like a well-traveled man." It's an odd greeting, but Leonidas smiles. It's a lot easier, he reflects, to feel comfortable with Brimelow's menacing presence looming just behind him.

"I suppose," Leonidas says, "that is true. I have had occasion to see a fair piece of the West but not this fair piece. This is my first time in Great Salt Lake City."

"Most of the folk here just call it Salt Lake City— or Salt Lake."

"My first time in Salt Lake City, then."

The man thrusts his shovel into the disheveled soil at the bottom of the grave and climbs out. "Jebediah Scrimm," he says and offers one muddy hand to Leonidas, who stares at him until he lowers it again.

"Pleased to meet you, Mr. Scrimm," Leonidas says. "I am Leonidas Pyburn."

"That'll be *Mr. Pyburn* to you," Brimelow growls, and Scrimm rewards him with an inquisitive, unimpressed stare.

"Mr. Pyburn," Scrimm says at length, "being as you are a visitor to our Territory, and thus live outside its peculiar strictures, I would ask you: have you any tobacco?"

Leonidas slides a slender gold-edged case from a vest

pocket and pops it open. Inside are a dozen or so hand-rolled cigarettes, redolent with the sweet, mellow scent of tobacco. He hands one to Scrimm and one to Brimelow and takes one for himself. Brimelow retrieves a battered box of matches from his coat pocket and pops one alight. The three men crowd companionably around Brimelow's flame, and soon they are smoking in comfortable silence. Scrimm breaks the spell. "This is good tobacco, Mr. Pyburn. It's not a habit I'm proud of, but we all have our failings, yes?"

"I have heard," Leonidas says, "that the religious and civil authorities of this Territory are not partial to tobacco, nor to spirits, nor to coffee or tea." Brimelow snorts at this but adds nothing. After leveling his curious stare at Brimelow for a few unnerving seconds, Scrimm replies.

"That's an apt way of putting it, yes. 'Not partial to tobacco,' yes, that's about right."

"It must be quaint, to live in a place so regulated by the laws of the spirit world."

"'The spirit world?' I'm not quite sure I follow, sir."

Leonidas blows thick white smoke from his nostrils and

rolls his words carefully on his tongue before giving them voice. "'Matters not temporal,' then? I have heard that your Prophet receives revelations directly from the Almighty and then passes them on to the city fathers. And that even the design of your city's streets was gifted to the Saints in a vision."

The gravedigger smokes in silence, weighing his own words as carefully as Leonidas had weighed his. Eventually, he pinches the end of his cigarette out with callused fingers. It is extinguished in a shower of sparks. "'Matters not temporal.'" Scrimm slips the remaining, unsmoked three-quarters of a cigarette into his pocket. "Being as you are a visitor here, I should ask you if you've heard the tale of Jean Baptiste."

"Hmmm. No, I can't say I've heard that name."

The gravedigger's leathery face is split by a broad grin, which displays a mouth full of strong, white teeth. "Well now," says Scrimm. "It's a story you'll want to hear, I'd wager."

¤

"Jean Baptiste was a drifter. He washed up here in Salt Lake City almost twenty years ago and got himself a job

111

right here in the Cemetery as a gravedigger—don't ask *me* how. The first graves were laid in here in fall of 1848, and there was work aplenty to be had digging final resting places for the dead in those early days; there still is. Baptiste made good. He built himself a little house right near the edge of the Cemetery. Married a woman named Dorothy. Even led the choir in his ward—that's a regular congregation of Latter Day Saints, for you gentiles.

"The War Between the States started in 1861, if you'll recall. What you probably *don't* recall is that the Yanks were forced to withdraw the Union Army from Utah Territory to fight the Rebs. By winter, the Shoshone began harrowing our northernmost settlements and threatening the telegraph lines that had just been erected that very year. The Church had seized control of the Territory by then, and they sought to restore order, but we soon learned that even the Church can't yet muster the manpower that the United States Army enjoys. We were sorely vexed by the Shoshone, and soon enough, many of us were desperate for the Army's return, although when it came in 1862, we would regret at leisure what we had desired in haste.

"The winter that stretched out between '61 and '62 was bitter, the ground as hard as marble— trust me, I know from doing this job longer than anyone ought to that January is the hardest month to sink a grave. That doesn't stop folks from dying, of course, but you hope for an easy winter when that freeze creeps in and turns the soil to iron. So, it was that January of '62, when Jean Baptiste planted that poor fool Moroni Clawson six deep in a cheap casket. Clawson was killed by the police after he had joined in on the beating of Governor Dawson.

"Oh, close up your mouth and don't gape at me, Mr. Brimelow. Governor Dawson was no Saint and conducted himself as such toward a woman of excellent repute. The imbroglio took place on New Years' Eve and was undoubtedly the product of Dawson's weakness for spirits, one that was almost as pronounced as his weakness for comely women. His reward was severe, no doubt— Moroni was not the only man to lay into Dawson, nor was Dawson beset only once. Broken bones and bruises were his payment, and he beat a hasty retreat from our Territory and was seen no more. Moroni Clawson, being a rough man of ill temper, put the police to the test when they went to collect him, and they answered with swift bullets, and that was the end of his story.

"Or so we thought.

"A stranger paid for Clawson's burial as an act of Saintly charity, and into the hard ground he went, tucked into his eternal rest by the good Jean Baptiste. And good he may have remained in our estimation, no doubt of that, if the Clawson family hadn't come up from Draper to exhume and collect Moroni's body for reburial at a family plot far south of the City. Jean Baptiste was unusually scarce when the Clawson men set to turning up Moroni with shovels, and that was wise, on Baptiste's part.

"For, you see, when they pried open Moroni's casket, they found him stuffed into his coffin face down— face down and as naked as the day he was born. It was an outrage. You see, when Christ returns and brings his Kingdom to the Earth, He shall raise the dead, that they may greet him with glad, resurrected hearts. The saintly dead will rise, be sure of that, and they shall rise clad as they were clad in the grave, temple garments, jewels, and restored flesh alike. To rob someone of that dignity— to make them greet Christ naked and ashamed— it is beyond blasphemous. It flies in the face of everything we believe about the grave and what waits for us beyond it. It was an act of monstrous desecration.

"Now, Officer Heath of the Salt Lake City Police Department— who had paid for Moroni's burial clothes— took the Clawson men with him to the sexton's house, where they demanded to know what on Earth was going on. The sexton said he knew nothing and further said that the men should talk to Jean Baptiste, the gravedigger. The ward had taken Baptiste to its collective bosom, him being an immigrant with bad English (where he came from, nobody knows— some say he was French, but evidently he spoke Italian, so who can say). This is how he had repaid their generosity of spirit?

"At Jean Baptiste's house, they found no Jean Baptiste. They *did* find box upon box of clothes, some still befouled by grave dirt, others already half-cleaned and readied for resale at shops throughout the City. The men tracked Jean Baptiste

115

down in the Cemetery, doing his labor in the frozen soil and the bitter cold, and Officer Heath confronted him. 'Yes,' Jean Baptiste confessed, weeping, 'It is true. I have done it. Spare my life. Please, my life. Please.' The scoundrel was taken into custody right there, amidst the graves, and secreted to the jail before the Saints of Salt Lake could learn what he had done and muster a mob to do vengeance to him. When Heath and others began to scrutinize Baptiste's previous doings, it turned out that Baptiste had violated hundreds of graves. *Hundreds.*

"President Brigham Young— our American Moses— showed Jean Baptiste truly Christlike mercy. He reasoned with our temporal leaders and the police and spared Baptiste the firing squad. Indeed, even a life imprisoned behind bars was not to be his fate. We could not suffer him to live in our midst; all President Young's wisdom wouldn't spare him a mob execution, were he released to his own recognizance. So the City employed a punishment more fashionable in the days of Nephi than today. Jean Baptiste was exiled.

"Exiled into the Great Salt Lake to Fremont Island, a miserable little spit of mud and grass inhabited for part of the year by a herd of cattle. He was marooned on that gloomy island, shackled to an iron ball to prevent his swimming to freedom (and the shore, it should be said, looks tantalizingly close from the Island, I'd warrant). The island was already home to a little wooden shack built by the cowherds with which he managed to keep the rain off of his head. After two days, some men from the City rowed out to him with charitable provisions, and they noted the wildness of his eyes, his matted hair, his slack and drooling mouth. He was beginning to degenerate already.

"A week after that, the unlucky men selected for the task piloted their little rowboat to Fremont Island and found Jean Baptiste shut up in his shack, weeping. 'The dead,' he said to them. 'The dead are here with me. *Vengono di notte*. At night, *capisci*?' I happen to speak adequate Italian; I haven't always lived here in Deseret. 'They come at night,' is what he was trying to tell them. He became agitated, and Officer Heath— who had volunteered for this excursion— had to lay him out with his fists. So there he was marooned, and there, the thinking was, he would stay, contained but not confined, shackled but alive. As it turned out, old Jean Baptiste still had one more twist left in him.

"A month into the grave robber's exile, the party again rowed out to re-provision the prisoner. This time, he was no-where to be seen— and nor was the wooden shack. As near as the men could figure, Jean Baptiste had torn the shack apart and used the wooden slats to build a crude raft capable of bearing both his weight and the weight of his iron ball. Out into the lake he went, and thus, to freedom. Or so they thought until just last year, when a pair of brothers hunting near the Lake's shallows found a salt-bleached skull. A little exploration turned up a set of leg-bones still anchored to the Lakebed by the iron ball where it had pulled Jean Baptiste to his death.

"There are those who think his end fitting and ironical, a bid for freedom that ended when Heavenly Father saw fit to end his miserable life. Not me, no, sir. I suspect that Jean Baptiste was chased off of his island by the dead. The dead who came at night."

Chapter Six

When Scrimm has finished his tale, a half-smile plays upon his lips as he gauges their reaction. Brimelow, for his part, issues a disgusted-sounding grunt. Leonidas takes a final drag on his cigarette and drops it to the ground, where he delicately stubs out its glowing end with the pointed tip of his shoe. "Jean Baptiste the supposed Italian, you say. The scum that wash up on the shores of this fair land are a burden that I'm not entirely sure we should be forced to bear," Leonidas says, and he savors the bitter taste of smoke that lingers on his tongue as he does. "America for Americans is what I say. Mind you, I say that as a man who has had to make use of foreign labor of many types. Let me tell you, Mr. Scrimm— I have seldom been other than cheated by the mangy curs, the exploitative blood-suckers who swarm our borders and infest our blessed soil. But the sewer grates are open, whether I like it or not, and this rich, beautiful land will soon, no doubt, be flooded by heathen Chinese, feral Irishmen, and swarthy Roman Papists."

Scrimm offers no reply to this. He bends carefully and fishes the last half-inch of Leonidas' cigarette from the dirt and slips it into the pocket of his threadbare coat.

Leonidas breathes in the warm air through his nose and savors the taste: green grass, freshly turned earth, some flowering tree whose perfume permeates even the expansive lawns of the Cemetery. Once, he would have found his contemplation of the scene untroubled, soothing, even. Now, one thought displaces all others: *This acreage is wasted on the dead— all this peace, the lovely lawns, utterly wasted.* That the pastoral environment is a nod to the aesthetic hungers of the living is not lost on him. No, the stark truth is that Leonidas wants grief to hurt, wants it to bite deep with its poison fangs. Death has, for too long, been swathed in the noxious, reeking vapor of comfort.

"Hmmm. I would like to ask you a question if I may, Mr. Scrimm. Your work brings you out here among the graves often, I assume."

"Every day. Some nights, too."

"Have you, in the course of your duties, seen anything… *unusual* of late? Anything that reminded you of Jean Baptiste? Graves desecrated, that sort of thing?"

"Unusual?" The gravedigger regards Leonidas with his bright, curious little eyes for a long moment. "No, Mr. Pyburn, I can't tell you that I've seen anything *unusual*. Aside from *you*, of course. And desecrations, sir? On *my* watch?"

"Me?" Leonidas scoffs. "Unusual? How do you mean?"

"Well, sir, would I be correct in assuming that you do not have people buried here? No family numbered among our guests?"

"Hmmm. You are correct in that, as it happens."

"Perhaps a friend, or some old partner in an undertaking from the War? But no, I think not."

121

Leonidas is silent.

"Then why," asks Scrimm, leaning on the handle of his shovel, "are you haunting my bone-yard, listening to my ramblings, asking questions about 'anything unusual' and *desecrations*?" He chuckles. "You look like an important man, Mr. Pyburn, at least in the earthly sense. What are you *doing* here?"

"You just watch yourself with the questions," Brimelow snarls. The big man steps casually from behind Leonidas and nearer to Scrimm. His chest puffs out, and his hands—with their hard, scarred knuckles and thick fingers— squeeze themselves into fists.

"Mr. Brimelow," Leonidas admonishes in a gentle tone.

"I suppose," he says to Scrimm, "I have taken up enough of your day. I can see that you have work you'd best attend to. Thank you, Mr. Scrimm— it has been a pleasure to make your acquaintance."

"Likewise, I suppose." Scrimm pulls the shovel from the ground with a grunt and sets to work again excavating the black earth of a new grave.

¤

Silence settles over Leonidas and Brimelow as they pick their way back through the stones to the carriage, a silence that lingers through the last few blocks of their journey. The houses that surround the graveyard are small, neat things, meticulously framed and shingled, and each surrounded by a nascent garden and yard, in which green things are just beginning to take root and thrive. They are still sparse, these little oases of domestic peace, but Leonidas can see beams rising against the dark evening blue of the spring sky and can hear the persistent staccato percussion of hammers. It's a community just beginning to take root, he thinks, and who is to say what it will blossom into? Would it become a fruiting tree or an acrid, poisonous shrub? He supposes that, ultimately, it's none of his concern. He does not intend to stay in Great Salt Lake City for long, no matter how pleasant the warm, dry air is, nor how intoxicating the bustling energy of its budding industries and commerce may be. And they are intoxicating. The dynamo of capital, Leonidas has discovered, generates a hum to which he has become almost supernaturally attuned, and he feels its thrum and pulse in the bones of the young city where his son has made his home. *Is it the silver?* He wonders. There's *something* here bending the arc of prosperity in the direction of the Mormon homeland; he can *feel* it.

Perhaps his son can as well, at least in some neutered way, for here he has made his home—and, as it turns out, Miles *does* have a lovely home. Leonidas' recent communique to Miles had been the first open contact attempted in decades, but the elder Pyburn *has* quietly kept tabs on his black sheep. (*Black sheep*, he sneers to himself silently. *More of a wooly white little lamb.*) The skies in his lamb's adopted city provide no shortage of supernatural backdrops; the coach pulls up before Miles' house just as twilight is beginning to brush the foothills above the city in shades of deep, regal purple. The house—*the Pyburn house, or one of them, anyway*, Leonidas corrects himself—shines like a jeweler's display, all brilliant golden light through well-paned windows. The front door even has a diminutive, lead-framed square of stained glass cut into it, a cunning touch that sends a spray of rubies and emeralds over the porch and down the front steps. It must be, he decides, a comforting sight to come home to, a warm-looking (if snug) little patch of peace in a corner of North America that had managed, somehow, to remain unscathed by the war that had driven the young nation to the brink of calamity. *There have been*, Leonidas thinks, *difficulties in this Territory, to be sure. The Governor beaten within an inch of his life—? What sort of people* are *these*? But, he had to admit, there were no cannon scars on the buildings here, no abattoir-tents full of shrieking amputees, no cities burned to cinders or looted as if by rampaging Goths. Maybe a Governor or two beaten half to death could have turned the United States aside from war. *Realistically*, he concludes, *no— sometimes blood* must *be shed. Sometimes* oceans *of blood must be shed.*

Leonidas mounts the steps with grim-faced vigor, Brimelow following—as always— a few steps behind his left shoulder. He raps on the doorframe with the gold head of his cane, which produces a sharp, reverberant knock. Leonidas has just enough time to straighten his vest and adjust his whiskers before the door opens, sending a pool of warm, yellow light across the yard. Framed by this cheerful glow is a man with a midsection softening to a distinguished paunch. His face is wreathed by a long, well-maintained beard as black as night. His broad forehead shines: *Miles*.

When he sees his father, Miles' face is creased by a smile of genuine joy, which sets the deep lines and wrinkles of his face into sharp relief. *My God, he has gotten old*, marvels Leonidas, and this is followed by another, more familiar thought: *How old have I become? And how many days can I have left?* "Father!" cries Miles, and before Leonidas is fully aware of what is happening, he is folded into a hearty, meaty embrace, held hard against Miles' rather doughy chest and the swell of his belly. Overcome by paternal instinct, Leonidas returns the embrace. He is surprised by the sudden rush of ridiculous tears that rise in his throat. He fights a brief— but victorious— battle to keep them out of his voice.

"Miles," he says, "Hmmm. It's been a long time, son."

"A long time," marvels Miles. "Father, it has been *twenty-two years*."

"Yes, well." Leonidas shifts on his feet, embarrassed.

"Hmmm. As I said, a long time."

"Please, come in; come in!" Miles' crinkle-faced enthusiasm is infectious, and even Brimelow offers him a thin and reluctant smile that is uncharacteristically shy. Miles takes their coats and hangs them in a front closet, which Leonidas notices is crammed almost to bursting with items ranging from a toddler's woolen sweater to a stout man's frock coat. The house's floors are a happy chaos of wooden toys, which Miles— now having his turn at embarrassment— rushes to push out of sight. Beyond the foyer, the living room is full of children, all engaged in an excited babble of conversation that leaves Leonidas feeling a bit spooked. He counts six of them, ranging in age from, yes, twin toddlers, up to a boy of about fourteen, a serious, quiet lad whom Miles introduces as Lehi. Before long, Miles' wife appears, new babe in arms. *That makes seven*, marvels Leonidas. "This," says Miles with obvious pride and affection, "is my wife Temperance."

"Hmmm. A name fit for a Mormon princess, I'd wager— unless you, by chance, happen to *have* spirits in the house?" Leonidas may as well have upturned a bucket full of scorpions onto the living room rug. A hush falls over the Pyburn children, and in what seems like only moments, Temperance has whisked all of them but Lehi from the room without so much as a word to or glance at Miles' father. Miles clears his throat.

"We are members of a community in Christ, father. I'm glad to have you here. More glad than you know, in fact, and we have much to speak of, no doubt. But if you cannot keep a civil tongue in your head and respect the doctrines by which we live our life, I'm afraid that your visit will be short indeed."

"Easy," says Brimelow from behind Leonidas, and the black undercurrent of violence has returned to his voice. "He was just asking if you have any drink. It has been a long trip from California."

"No. We have nothing like that in our home."

"Pity," says Brimelow, and that appears to constitute the sum of his interest in anything that Miles has to say. He retires to a wooden chair near the entrance to the living room and sets to cleaning his black fingernails with the pointed tip of a rather extravagant dagger.

"I'm afraid that you've missed dinner." Miles' tone is polite, chilly, and stiff, and Leonidas suspects that if he had not made sport (even such gentle sport) of Temperance or the family's religious strictures, dinner may have been in the offing. *No matter*, he thinks.

"I stopped at the City Cemetery on the way here, Miles. I must say, it's as orderly as the graves that I remember from Winter Quarters."

"Ah. Yes." If possible, Miles' voice has become even more formal, more laden with ice.

"I had a chance," Leonidas continues, probing, "to speak with a very loquacious gravedigger. He shared— with Mr. Brimelow and myself—the story of a fellow named Jean Baptiste. If there were any truth in his account, it must have been quite the to-do."

"Oh, yes. If he told you the story of Jean Baptiste, the criminal, the grave-robber and desecrator, the cuckoo's egg taken into the nest of my very ward, then yes, he told you true."

129

"*Really*. Hmmm. He was banished, then? To a little mud island in that great inland sea?"

"He was shown," Miles says, his words careful, "tremendous mercy. Mercy of which it would be difficult for a gentile to conceive. Believe me, father, when I tell you that Jean Baptiste's true punishment did not come in this world. He will be cast in death to Outer Darkness."

"I must ask, resurrectionists have been plying their trade in England for a hundred years," says Leonidas. "While more than one man has swung for his crimes against the dead, I don't think I ever detected in the stories I heard from my miners in those early days the anguish that you Saints seem to find in the bothering of the dead." This last is pronounced with a sincerity that thaws a bit of the ice in Miles. The portly Pyburn prodigal stares at his father, measuring him with bright blue eyes.

"We, of the restored Church of Jesus Christ, know many things that would surprise you, father. Do you remember the last conversation we had before parting ways at South Pass?"

"Hmmm. Of course. You told me that you planned to

follow the Saints. And I will give you this much, boy: you followed through on your plans. Whether I agree with your spiritual notions or not, you are not a man who can be turned aside once he sees a life he wants." *Perhaps there's a bit of me in this tubby paterfamilias after all,* Leonidas thinks. "Your lovely wife and children, including, hmmm, young Lehi here, make your case for you well enough."

"Lehi is not so young. He is here because he is a man and a member of the Priesthood. He can listen to men speak; I'd like him to hear his grandfather's words for himself." Miles wrings his big hands, the knuckles still scarred from his days as a pugilist. "One of the things which I said to you at South Pass was that I was drawn to the possibilities implied by eternal progression beyond death. I know now that my curiosity on that subject was the fruit borne by the promptings of the Holy Spirit, leading me to the Land of Zion, here in the bosom of Deseret."

"Yes. Well." Now it is Leonidas' voice that has become stilted and laced with ice.

"Being as," continues Miles, "we believe in the eternal

131

progression of the spirit— and the resurrection of the flesh, to be clad as we are interred, restored to glorious perfection—we take the crime of desecration very seriously. It has been a long time, father, since these secrets of the grave were lost by the Tribes of Israel. Now they have been restored to us. Your business ventures must keep you abreast of events back East. Have you heard much of the exhibits that have come through North America from Egypt?"

"Oh," says Leonidas quietly, "I may have heard a thing or two about Egypt."

"Long millennia after their deaths, the Pharaohs of old have finally landed here, where Eden once thrived— where Nephi set foot long ago. The arrival of their mummies is not without import; many things have come to pass of late which speak of great forces at play upon the Earth. The ancient Egyptians too believed in the eternal progression of the soul, did you know that, father? Although they were a heathen culture that worshiped false gods. Perhaps, in their long and regal slumber in their splendid cerements, the Pharaohs have progressed beyond the fate assigned them by their idolatry.

132

Have you heard of the Prophet Joseph Smith's translation of Reformed Egyptian?"

"That," says Leonidas, "I am not familiar with. 'Reformed Egyptian' may still be, hmmm, the stuff of revelation, rather than scholarship."

Excitement has climbed into Miles' voice like a flourishing vine, upon which bloom the sparkling blue flowers of his eyes. "There is so much we have to learn yet from those tombs, those relics of ancient days of Israelite bondage. Here— you, perhaps more than any other man I have known, will appreciate this." Miles stands and walks to a tall bookcase in one corner of the room. When he turns back to Leonidas, he holds a small leather book whose cover is embossed with a symbol that is unmistakably of the ancient Egyptian type. He flips through it until he reaches a dog-eared page in the middle and then hands it to his father, who reads the tilt-stamped title before opening it to the marked passage: *Being an Encyclopedia of Egyptian, Arab, and Persian Myth.*

"Read," says Miles, and Leonidas does.

Ghūl – Taker. Dweller in dead places. Feaster on corpseflesh.

133

Plague of the tomb that spreads foulness where it makes its home. Bringer of malady. Mindless hunger of the not-dead, not-living. Twisted longbones, which seeks after human offal. Sickener. Haunter of tombs and destroyer of cities. Grave-worm that grubs in the sand. Shadow which shuns the sun which burns with purifying fire, the merciless sun which consumes that which cannot be healed. Ghūl: eater of rot.

"Hmmm." Leonidas passes the book back to Miles, eager to have it out of his hands as quickly as possible. He finds the touch of its leather cover unpleasantly warm, as though the small volume were a living thing, something waiting for an opportunity to bite him with vicious fangs. "You read this, and you thought of Abner."

"Yes," agrees Miles, "Abner."

The silence that follows this exchange feels flammable, dangerous. "I think I would enjoy a cigarette and a breath of the crisp evening air, if you wouldn't mind me stepping outside for a few moments," Leonidas says and climbs to his feet with more difficulty than he would have preferred to display. "Mister Brimelow will keep me company."

"I will join you as a matter of fact." For a moment, Miles sounds like the young man he had once been, brash, trapped in his father's shadow and overwhelmed with love for him at the same time. "Lehi will stay here. Mr. Brimelow can do as he wishes."

"Mr. Brimelow," Brimelow says, "would stay in here where it's warm, if it's all the same to you, Mr. Pyburn."

Coats and hats in place, Miles and Leonidas step outside and detour around the back of the house. The green swath behind the Pyburn house is dotted with young cherry trees. As Brimelow had feared, the air has taken on an evening nip that feels sharp to Leonidas, an adopted son of the California coast. He doesn't even attempt to mask his surprise when, as he plucks a cigarette from his gold case, Miles reaches for one. "I was under the impression that you Saints viewed the indulgence of tobacco as a sin. Yet, since I've arrived here, my little gold case here has scarcely closed. It's fortunate for the good people of sin-starved Salt Lake City that I'm so generous."

"Tobacco is against the Word of Wisdom. Alas, it appears

135

I am a sinner after all." This flash of his old cynical sense of humor is followed by the flash of a struck match in the dark. As Miles holds up the flame and the two men light their cigarettes, there is a moment of shared inhalation and enjoyment, a luxury shared in the cooling darkness beyond the warm ring of light outside the Pyburns' kitchen window. Each of them bears, in his hands, a tiny dot of Promethean fire, a private charm against the night.

Leonidas speaks first. "I was worried, while I was listening to the story of Jean Baptiste, that Abner may have had something to do with it. Bodies meddled with... the City Cemetery here, so big and so full of dead. I was worried that he'd been drawn here by the banquet and then come to an end even more terrible than..."

"Than what we did to him?" Miles asks. His tone is no longer ice; it now has a saber's edge. "Than being abandoned to die, to starve in a godforsaken ghost town?"

"Miles, we don't *know* what happened to Abner. Not for certain."

"Abner is dead."

"We don't *know* that, Miles!"

"Abner is dead," Miles says. "I know it because I killed him myself."

Chapter Seven

"What in God's name are you talking about, Miles?"

"Nothing I did was in God's name back then, not yet. I was led through the shadow of the valley of death by the Lord without knowing His face," Miles says. "Come, sit, and I will tell you of Abner's death." He sits down with a grunt and a sigh upon a long, rough-hewn bench adjoining a wooden work table, and Leonidas joins him.

"Do you remember," Miles asks, "the storm after we parted ways at South Pass?"

"Hmmm. Yes. I managed to avoid the worst of it by making good time to the West."

"I see. I did not avoid it, for I had business to attend to before I followed the Saints to this valley." Miles clears his throat. "It was bloody business." With that preamble, Miles begins to speak. His voice is sorrowful, but the words come with steady assurance, and Leonidas listens, mesmerized.

¤

(1848)

When Miles and Leonidas part ways at South Pass, the clouds come thick and as black as smoke. The rain lasts for two days, a steady, heavy drizzle that washes over the grass plains like a misplaced ocean. Miles is glad of it and only half-heartedly looks for shelter. He wishes to be scoured. In the end, though, the water drenching his coat and rolling off the brim of his hat in a torrent doesn't offer any absolution. The ordeal only serves to make his horse miserable. Miles cannot wash the taste of grave dirt off of his tongue or chase the stench of rotting human flesh from his nostrils. It takes him less than a day to reach a decision.

His return trip to the ghost town goes by more quickly than Miles is entirely prepared for. After a tectonic recalibration of wind and cloud, the sun reemerges from the days-long shroud of thunderheads. It bakes the sodden mud of the grass plain to a hard, brown crust, and the return of birdsong is riotous in the sweet-smelling air. Miles' spirits, however, do not lift with the return of daylight, though it makes his reconnaissance of the ghost town easier than it might have been in the gloom. Miles hobbles his horse a short walk from the perimeter of the derelict town and approaches its boundaries with careful, quiet steps.

It has been three days— maybe four— since Leonidas and Miles left Abner in the cellar of the abandoned house. In that time, Abner has been industrious, to judge by the many tracks left in the drying mud and the terrible evidence of violent exhumations that Miles observes in the little town's graveyard. Miles has traveled light. Other than his rifle and a kerchief tied around his neck, all of his preparations for this return visit to the root cellar fit neatly into the burlap sack that he carries over one shoulder and which issues an occasional soft, metallic clink. Miles picks his careful way through the deserted town to the empty house where he and his father had left Abner only days before. Could it really, Miles marvels, have been less than two weeks since Christiansen's intrusion on the Pyburn campsite and the subsequent parade of death to which they had been subjected? He supposes, calculating with foggy distraction, that that has to be correct.

There is another story that Abner's long, misshapen footprints tell, stamped in the mud. While most of them have beaten a path directly from house to graveyard, there are also prints that wander through the streets of the ghost town. Abner, it seems, had been searching for something— and Miles cannot shake the notion that what Abner had been hunting for had been his missing father and absent brother. Miles stops outside of the house, whose cellar had housed what was left of his only sibling, the diminished other half of a matched fraternal set. His internal struggle is brief, silent, and violent, but in the end, he manages to rake together his courage and straighten his spine. *I will not leave my brother here, to root among the dead and go to rot*. The thought is a single flame that blazes pure in his mind and burns away his

141

fear and disgust. He sets his bag carefully on the ground and rummages in it until he finds what he's looking for.

First, he withdraws a great, fierce knife (almost a sword, really) wrapped in a leather sheath, which he ties to one thigh. The knife had been bought in half-jest to celebrate the trip west into the wilderness with his father and brother, but he's glad to have it now for purely practical reasons. It's just short of a foot long and razor-sharp. This attended to, he withdraws a handful of cartridges, one of which he uses to load his rifle; the rest go into his shirt pocket. *There is no room for mistakes this time*, he thinks. He has already decided that if Abner bites him—if he too is sickened by whatever ungodly affliction this is— he will have to take his own life. He does not dread the possibility as much as he might have a mere month ago.

With his rifle loaded and slung over his shoulder, Miles retrieves another item from his bag, one which had been Abner's until his dispossession: a hooded oil lantern with red leaded glass and a long, curved handle. Lantern lit and in hand (but with its tin shutters closed) and rifle prepared,

Miles steps over the threshold of the house. He winces at the long, shivering creak that reverberates through its empty rooms as soon as he applies his weight to the wooden floor-boards. *No matter*, he thinks. *If Abner is asleep, he will sleep through my approach. If he is awake, I am most likely doomed already if he is as strong and as fast as that wretch in Winter Quarters.*

The house is not entirely silent, Miles soon perceives; there is a low, atonal hum in the air, a vibrato murmur that he can't quite place. Other than the sound, there is no sign of life, certainly no sign of Abner. Not in the main part of the house, but then, Miles did not expect to find anything aboveground, where the sun's ferocious rays even now shine through the house's many windows. Miles shifts the kerchief around his neck up over his mouth and nose as he approaches the trapdoor to the cellar. The floor between the front door and the entry to the cellar is smeared with long, muddy footprints—and a single handprint is stamped upon the lid of the trapdoor as clearly as if it had been left deliberately. Miles' mind turns up an unexpected memory: his mother, reading "Red Riding Hood" to her young sons. *Oh Abner*, thinks Miles, *what long fingers you have. "The better to pluck at dainties."*

Miles shudders and pulls the trapdoor open. It reveals a square of pitch darkness out of which billows the foulest stench that Miles has ever had the misfortune of experiencing. The kerchief helps a bit, but the smell is strong enough that Miles has to rip the cover from his face so that he can vent an explosive jet of vomit to one side of the trapdoor. *If Abner didn't hear that*, thinks Miles, *he is well and truly dead to the world.*

Miles steps over the splatter of his vomitus and places one boot, then another, on the rungs of the ladder that leads down to the cellar. He descends slowly, carefully, silently, into a carrion darkness thick with the smell of death and excrement. The sound that he had detected through the floorboards turns out to be the buzzing of a veritable inferno of flies, a black, riotous cloud of chaos that buffets Miles' face. If they had tracked the thing in the Winter Quarters cemetery back to its lair, would they have discovered foulness to equal—nay, to exceed, even—this? Miles suspects so, for what agency other than pure instinct could possibly be driving Abner at this point? *This is Hell,* he thinks as he descends, near-delirious with fear. *Right here on Earth, and I damned Abner to it with my cowardice. Whatever my fate today, as God as my witness, I will release my brother.*

As he reaches the bottom of the ladder, Miles' boot skates off of something hard that rolls away in the dark, tracing a lopsided trajectory. He holds stock-still for a moment and listens. Below the churning, atonal music of the flies, he can make out another sound: a regular, sonorous snore, hard to mistake for anything other than the breath of a deep slumber. *Dead to the world after all,* Miles marvels, then corrects himself: *Would something dead breathe so deeply in its sleep, if indeed the dead sleep?* He thinks not. He thinks the damnation that has claimed Miles is a morbid, twilit fate that lies somewhere between death and life. There is a smell of corruption in the cellar, to be sure, but it is a stench with an animal undertone. If he'd thought the smell of the cellar foul when he had opened the trapdoor, he now finds it almost unbearable.

145

It is a thick and viscous thing, an all-permeating stain of rotten flesh and sewage and beastly foulness: part chamber pot, part open grave, and all undershot by something harder to identify, something that has in it a touch of madness. How had this place grown so foul in only a few days? Miles suspects he knows the answer: Abner has been bringing home treasures to enjoy here, in the cellar that has become both his bed and privy.

Miles—careful of the hinges— opens the lantern until a single slender ray falls upon the floor of the cellar and confirms his suspicion. The floor is littered with human bones. Many of them are denuded in their entirety, but a few still bear hunks and chunks of rotten meat. The light that creeps through the leaded glass is a deep crimson, and as the lantern trembles in Miles' shaking hands, it casts a lone, shivering beam against the far wall of the cellar. The effect is not unlike being inside a great, cavernous heart pumping dark blood through some unimaginable body. This jigging of the light reveals the answer to one mystery as the beam plays over the floorboards that form the cellar's roof: all the chinks and cracks in the boards which might admit light or allow the wet warmth of Abner's nest to escape have been plugged, sealed over with dried and drying excrement. This night-soil basilica has hardened to a protective shell, which has banished the light and trapped the cellar's heat and moisture (and bouquet). *This ghastly cave,* thinks Miles, *has become Abner's outhouse, larder, and bedroom, all in one. This is how a beast lives.* Indeed, Miles has heard tell of animals in the swamps far away in the South that haul their prey underwater to secret pantries where the carcasses are allowed to rot until they soften and grow ripe for the bog-predator's delectation. Miles, again, fights with his stomach and this time wins. *You can vomit again,* he tells himself, *when this is done.*

Miles concentrates and stills the trembling in his hands enough to play the lantern's thin light around the cellar. It's a most unpleasant search, carried out in blood-colored half-darkness, but after a moment, he sees what he is looking for: a hole burrowed into a back corner of the room. The mouth of the hole is an epicenter of scattered bones. They fan out in profusion before it, picked and sucked clean. Miles ap-

147

proaches the burrow with careful steps and avoids scattering any more of the calcified treats. When he is a few paces from the entrance to the little den— from which the snores that fill the cellar issue—he stops and lifts his lantern, casting its ray of venous light into the depths.

At the bottom of the hole, which isn't deep, is Abner. His limbs are wrapped around his distorted, lengthened body as though to give himself comfort— but no comfort is evident in the eye that stares out at Miles, open but filmed and sightless in sleep. It is a vulture's eye, a thing clouded by the grotesque change worked upon Abner by the graveyard stalker's bite. It remains motionless behind its sightless skin, a repulsive sight in the lantern's ray, dull blue beneath a hideous veil. Miles sets the lantern carefully— so carefully—on the ground before the burrow, with its web-thin ray directed at the mouth. He shrugs his rifle off his shoulder and raises it with the chamber already loaded. *I am either in Hell*, he thinks, *or in the very heart of Death's vast mansion— and in the end, is there a difference?* The flies are a symphony of mindless, lunatic sound, conducted by the motionless limbs scattered about the floor, and for one moment, gazing into the hole at the very bottom of the cellar, the lair of the thing that had been his brother, Miles teeters giddily on the brink of madness.

What saves him— what pulls him back— is the knowledge that there is one final service he can perform for Abner, who is well and truly lost. Miles loosens the big knife in its sheath and then does his best to stifle his nerves and stop the tip of his rifle from trembling as he thumbs back his weapon's hammer. The metallic click of the action feels as loud in the confines of the cellar as the gunshot it precedes, and Miles winces, then waits… Nothing. No sound of wakefulness but no continuing snore, either. Miles wipes his forehead with one sleeve. In the warm, sodden air, he has begun to sweat.

Abner erupts, snakelike, from the mouth of his burrow and springs. His appearance unfolds without warning and without a sound: no growl, no bellow, barely so much as a ragged exhalation and the whisper of soil against bare sole. His blue, murky eyes roll like those of a great fish, and his jaws snap shut with a vicious *CLACK*. His misshapen man-

149

dibles deliver a bite that, had he had time to fasten it to his brother, would have ended the struggle before it had a chance to begin. Miles, however, in his nervous state, dwelt in the half-certainty that Abner would spring from his den, brings his rifle's sight to bear, smooth as silk, on the blue, clouded marble of his brother's left eye. It is a beautiful shot, clean through Abner's head, and as the ball exits his misshapen skull, it takes a great portion of his brains and no small fragment of bone with it.

In a sane world, Miles thinks, *one governed by any cosmic laws or sentience, none of this would have happened. Abner, father, and I would all be nearly to California by now.*

In one governed by a cruel Jehovah, he thinks, *I may have been forced to kill my brother.*

What world have I stumbled into, here in the West, where Abner lives on after such an injury? Where he snaps and bites with a jaw half-disassembled by a lead slug, with most of his brains missing? What drives things here, beyond the grave, reveling in rot beyond reason or Nature?

These thoughts fly through him with a cold clarity that is

like a killing, chilling wind in winter, one that cuts through the lush vegetation of his panic and revulsion and allows him, for the first time in his life, to act with something like total courage, an emptiness of all but pure purpose. He drops the rifle neatly and seizes it by the barrel in mid-air, swinging its wooden stock against Abner's ruined, half-diminished face so hard that the stock breaks with a brittle *CRACK!* The blow finishes dismantling Abner's lower jaw and sends a spray of broken, bloody teeth to the four winds. Somehow— Miles has no idea how— the horrible light of half-life persists in Abner's sole remaining eye, and though he staggers backward for a moment, the thing that had been Miles' brother continues to attack, scrabbling with desperate claws and an animalistic groan from deep in the exposed meat of his gullet.

The cold precision has not relinquished its hold on Miles, and he lets go of the rifle. Nimble as if he'd planned this maneuver for months, he pulls all eleven inches of his knife free and plunges it through Abner's heart. The momentum of the blow— and Miles' solid weight behind it— topple

Abner backward with his brother on top of him. The knife slides almost effortlessly through Abner, pinning him to the earth like an insect in an entomologist's specimen-box. Abner emits a sound that starts as a violent shriek, unfiltered by missing tongue or vanished jaw. It's so high-pitched it's almost out of Miles' hearing range. Then the sound of Abner's death agony fades as the air escapes his pierced lung, and it begins to fill with blood. Abner's long arms and naked, distorted legs engage in a violent scrabble, each limb like a jointed serpent. They flail and strike wildly. Abner's fingers—his claws, really—dig at the earth and slash at Miles, but Miles kneels atop him and holds him in place. The flies are a maelstrom around the two figures, stirred up by Abner's wild convulsions. Tears and snot run down Miles' face and dampen the kerchief. Abner dislodges great handfuls of the cellar's earthen floor as he flails. The earth itself down in the death-pit is unspeakably foul— moist with god-knows-what and redolent of rancid meat. The lantern tips over and shines red from a low angle, throwing a pandemonium of shadows onto the underside of the feces-caked floorboards above. *This* is *Hell*, Miles thinks again. His mind feels like it has exited his body through the top of his head; he feels like he is watching events unfold from a distance, his horror swaddled by detachment. *This is Hell*, he thinks, *and I've always been here, and I always will be. No eternal progression for me, just death and decay beneath the floorboards of the world, with this foul parody of my brother, whom I loved, locked in murder. It will always be this way, this moment: and I deserve it.*

Then a shudder runs through Abner, his bowels empty, and the life leaves his body. It is the single worst moment of Miles' life.

He rests for the space of a few ragged breaths, then returns to his feet and fetches the lantern from the floor. There's no point in keeping the shutter dimmed now, and Miles pulls it open to light his way to the ladder. He collects his burlap sack from the floor above, gulping in sweet mouthfuls of fresh air as soon as his head clears the boards. In contrast to the miasma in the cellar, the dusty night breeze that floats through the doorway is as intoxicating as wine. After recuperating, Miles withdraws his prizes from the burlap bag and returns to the dirt cave below with them tucked under his arm, where they slosh gently as he descends the ladder.

The night before his return to the ghost town, Miles had passed the dark and miserable hours camped in the lee of a rocky hill. His rest had been anxious and uneasy and had come sporadically, leaving him feeling unrefreshed. Sometime just before dawn, though, he had fallen into a deep slumber. He'd been drawn deep into a dream in which the stones of the hill had spoken to him with a voice like thunder. Had there been words in that vast, crashing chorus? His memory fails him, but Miles feels sure there hadn't been—that the stones had spoken in a way that felt far older than words. Regardless, the message had been clear and had followed him into wakefulness. *The only cure for this pollution is flame.* On waking, he had considered these words, remembering how the corpse of the graveyard-creeper in Winter Quarters had burned as though it were made of dry hay. Flame it would be, then.

In the foulness of the root cellar, Miles empties two flasks of lamp oil over the wooden beams. He then climbs back out and douses the floors of the house with the remaining flasks of oil. Finally, he tosses the lantern into the house from just beyond its entry. Before long, the house is completely cocooned in bright flames that send a black curtain of oily smoke into the clear blue of the afternoon sky. Miles sits beyond the ring of heat that pulses from the fire and watches the house burn until twilight falls. He thinks of what is being immolated: not just the wood of the house, but what lies beneath, hidden in the unspeakable darkness. He waits until the flames have consumed it utterly. Finally, the ashes and broken, smoldering chunks of wood collapse one upon the other as the whole mess sinks into the earth.

When it has finished burning, Miles stands and walks into the cool night beyond the ghost town.

Chapter Eight

Miles' words hang in the chilly air, rendered visible for a few moments by the clouds of his breath. The vapor drifts before him, beautiful in the moonlight, a ghostly presence there for only a passing instant and then gone forever. Leonidas says nothing for a long time— nearly a full minute— as he chews the words over. "Hmmm. It was an act of mercy in the end, wasn't it? You did the right thing, Miles."

"I don't doubt now that I did the right thing. However, I doubt, father, that *you* did the right thing, leaving Abner to feed on dead things in the dark, the only man in a hundred miles— but not a man at all, at that point, was he? The only

156

ghūl within a hundred miles, then. I know what *I* did was right. I do not mean I did right when I slew Abner, nor when I burned that clogged privy beneath that house and the house with it, nor when I remade the graves in that forsaken little town the next day, working until I sweat through my clothes to ensure that every grave was returned to the illusion of order, though they were, for the most part, empty. I stirred the ashes of the burned house and added more fuel, reigniting the fire for a time and burning the ashes even further until all the detritus in the cellar was immolated and mixed with the house's ash. In the end, the whole mess compacted in on itself like the socket left by a rotted tooth. No, none of that was a service to my brother. Abner is now at rest because of what came *later*, because of the intervention in my life of our Lord Jesus Christ and our Heavenly Father, the intervention that— eventually— brought me here."

Leonidas is surprised at how Miles' words— his matter-of-fact accusations—sting. "Hmmm. Well. Whatever one's beliefs, Abner can rest now."

"Certainly. His rest wouldn't be guaranteed for a time,

but I eventually made sure of it," Miles says and runs a hand over his face— broader and fleshier than Leonidas remembers it—and through his beard, then concludes his story. "I had just enough jerky and hardtack to keep me going until I found this place." He spreads his arms, as though to indicate that upon his arrival, it had all been waiting for him, warm and secure: his house, his wife, perhaps even his children. It's an absurd idea and a vast oversimplification. Leonidas' knowledge of Great Salt Lake City's history is spotty, but he has learned enough to know that it had been born—as all human habitations are— from blood, fire, and terror. Not the terror of open warfare (not yet, anyway), but terror nonetheless: land taken, disputes put down by bullet—the pedestrian terror of order.

"Hmmm. And I suppose you met Temperance here?"

"Eventually, yes. The first thing I did upon finding the early settlement here was to attend a church service. It was offered by what would become the ward I now serve on the Bishopric of. I encountered the Holy Spirit there, the first time I experienced a testimony of the truth of the Church.

158

The Lord spoke to me, in the stillness and silence within me, and revealed that the Prophet was, indeed, the restorer of the true Church and a worthy heir to the line of David, of Jesus, of the path of Peter." Miles' cigarette, long-since finished and stubbed out on the dirt, appears to suddenly irritate him, and he grinds it to bits viciously with the tip of his shoe. "I read the scriptures revealed to the Prophet and found truth in them, ringing in every word. I learned about the history of this great land and its destiny. I learned to humble myself before the Church and before Heavenly Father. It turns out that I was more right than I knew when I felt the pull of eternal progression, even for a creature like the one poor Abner had become. The Church possesses the keys of the Priesthood. We have offices—rites, although I can say little more— that assist a sinner even after his passage to the Telestial Kingdom. For example, we baptize by proxy."

"You what?"

"We perform baptisms for the dead." Miles' voice carries the patience of a parent teaching a very basic lesson to a particularly thick-headed child. "Those who undoubtedly need it the most. It is the revelation of this principle that most affirms my testimony that the Church is true."

"Hmmm." Leonidas feels embarrassed for Miles. His embarrassment sparks a surprising tenderness in his breast that wrestles with the contempt likewise kindled there. "I'll say this much, Miles: you have a lovely wife and a passel of fine-looking children."

"They are your grandchildren, father," Miles says. "Your blood. Your line."

This is a thought that is not unfamiliar to Leonidas. Indeed, it bears directly on his decision to come to Great Salt Lake City in the first place, thick though the trip be with the fetid stench of destiny. "They certainly are, Miles. I can see Pyburn stamped upon their faces— especially Lehi." Leonidas slips his pocket watch from his vest and checks the time. "I fear that I have another engagement to see to tonight before I retire. It was good to see you, Miles."

Miles is incredulous. "But you've just arrived! And my admission—what happened to Abner—"

What you did *to Abner*, Leonidas thinks, but what he says is: "I am only parting ways with you for the evening. I have business here that will keep me in town for a spell. When the time is right, you'll see me again." Leonidas stares out at the black well of the night beyond the glowing circle of light that rings Miles' house. "Believe you that, Miles: I will return."

¤

Leonidas collects Brimelow, and the two men make their valedictions to Miles and Temperance (the children have been, Leonidas notes with some relief, sent to bed). After Brimelow has retrieved his coat and hat, the big man and his employer make their way to the coach waiting on the street before the Pyburn house. The squash-faced driver retained for the evening has dozed off, snug inside his great woolen overcoat, but wakes with a startled snort when Brimelow opens the cab's door for Leonidas.

Their subsequent return trip to the city's budding downtown does not take long and is passed in weary silence by Brimelow and Leonidas— not a companionable silence, but one comfortable enough. The coach pulls up before the Delmonico Hotel, a tall stone building filled with light that spills in icy white profusion through its many windows. In the early evening, it is a veritable beehive of activity, a bustle of well-dressed men and women coming and going. *It's a beautiful building*, Leonidas reflects. *Doubly so for what it represents: the coming of Commerce to a would-be desert nation of religious zealots. More than politics, more even than soldiers bearing arms, it is Commerce that will bring this place to heel and enfold it to the bosom of the United States.*

"Good evening, Mr. Pyburn!" The front desk clerk's manner is obsequious, fairly larded with deference, and it irritates Leonidas to no end. His advance arrangements and reservations had unfortunately allowed his name—and the reputation of his wealth— to precede him, but such recognition still unsettles him. He utters a noncommittal grunt by way of reply, retrieves his key from the chattering clerk, and mounts the hotel's steps with a stiff, painful gait that is almost a limp by the time he reaches the penthouse. Brimelow, shepherding the bags from the carriage to their quarters, passes him a few times coming and going on the stairs. The silent, subtle insult inflicted by the sight of Brimelow's mobility only adds to Leonidas' foul mood.

Ensconced in his room, he checks his pocket watch again. Satisfied that he has arrived at his destination with time to spare, Leonidas retrieves a slim, leather-bound volume from his bags. Its title, stamped on the cover in tiny letters, reads *Dogme et Rituel de la Haute Magie* by Éliphas Lévi. Leonidas rests his aching joints and passes a quiet hour reading at the ornate desk in the room's corner. Brimelow stations himself in a chair beside the suite's door with his own selection of reading material: a battered paperback copy of *Luck and Pluck* by Horatio Alger Jr.

At length, a quiet knock comes, and Brimelow opens the door and admits a slender, dapper man. His face is unlined and almost boyish. From his immaculate and elaborate coif of blonde curls to his loud, checkered vest, knee-length velvet frock coat of royal purple, and spotless black boots, he is the very picture of a well-heeled and foppish young gentleman. He bears a walking stick in one hand, a simple, elegant thing of bright chestnut wood with a silver handle shaped like a raven's skull. His slender fingers are busy with rings of varying designs and metals. Some of the rings gleam with precious stones; others are scuffed and beaten-looking. All of them bear elaborate occult symbols: runes, the spidery shapes of sacred geometry etched in miniscule lines, tiny inscriptions in dead languages.

"Mr. Brimelow, Frater Leo Auream," he greets them in a clear, mellifluous voice. "I *do* hope that you have not had long to wait. *Such* a terrible bother, travel to these outposts, yes?" He favors them with a smile that lights his face with an androgynous beauty, though his eyes are an unsettling, glassy grey, and the deep creases and lines near their corners make his age, at a second glance, difficult to gauge. He could be a twenty-year-old man with a century-old soul, Leonidas has decided, or a hundred-year-old man with the stolen face of a youth. Either way, the slim man's manner conveys an unmistakable feeling of something unnatural at play.

"Frater Cygnus," Leonidas says in greeting. "No, we have not had long to wait. And per your distaste for out-of-the-way locales… You've enjoyed quite the leeway with your investigations, your *collection*, in remote corners, have you not? Have you ever had the same ease when you've had to confine your activities to the civilized world?"

"It *is* true that I've had more luck in Saqqara than I would have had in Cairo. That much I cannot deny."

"Hmmm. It's a lesson I learned in California. Best to do business in quiet places with few souls, whenever possible. The forgotten places are where a little lubrication and a pinch of persuasion can work true wonders." California had been a crucible that had re-forged Leonidas in unbreakable steel (or so he liked to tell himself). He hadn't developed a taste for blood there, per se, but he had lost whatever aversion to slit throats and crushed skulls he may have once had, along with the remnants of his natural empathy for those with less than he. Along the way, at some point— who is to say *precisely* the moment when such imaginary boundaries are crossed? —he had ascended the ranks of American wealth past the stations of "rich man" and "very rich man" to become one of his young nation's Olympian deities of accumulation. Pyburn had begun as a byword, a stand-in name for gold mining writ large. His operations had expanded since then to the extent that the name Pyburn now meant wealth unmoored from any specific industry or resource. His multifarious business ventures (*finance stacked upon finance*, he thinks, *so far removed from the precious metals I used to pull from the frozen stream with my bare hands*) now seemed perfectly capable of running themselves, like financial perpetual motion engines. Freed from such concerns, Leonidas turned his attention from the ethereal world of Capital to the ethereal world of the spirit.

When he had first developed this late-life fascination, he'd met numerous charlatans who had tried to exploit his interest in one way or another. He had made a point of allowing these would-be defrauders to go on their way unmolested after their dismissal— he figured that they performed a public service, fleecing the gullible and the stupid. Among the ranks of Spiritualists, tent-dwelling revivalists with sweat-drenched faces, and assorted mystics, there *were* a few— a very precious few— with real Talent. Some had been gifted by birth. Others developed their Talent through tremendous exertions of research, occult learning, and esoteric discovery.

166

Cygnus was, without a doubt, the most powerful mage that Leonidas had encountered in his wanderings. He had ascertained what it took to secure Cygnus' loyalty. The answer turned out to be opium (and other, more esoteric drugs, as well) and money, all of which Leonidas was only too happy to supply in whatever quantity was required to keep the strange, foppish man happy. Cygnus has now been his loyal servant almost as long as Brimelow. Like the big Irishman, Cygnus was a trusted part of the elder Pyburn's innermost circle. Outside of these trusted few, Leonidas' associates were mostly mercenaries, attorneys, fixers, and assorted sycophants and hangers-on.

"Did you just arrive?"

"No. I arrived yesterday. Be glad of that, too— I've had a chance to talk to the cemetery men."

"That," Leonidas replies, "was a waste of your time, no? I spoke to a gravedigger—one Mr. Scrimm— myself, and he reported nothing unusual. He *did* relay a rather charming story about an itinerant Italian, or possibly a Frenchman, named Jean Baptiste. A thief and a desecrator who met a

167

most untimely and horrible end, as such are wont to do. As charismatic as I found the character of Mr. Baptiste to be, I doubt very much that his tale has much bearing on our present goals. When I'd had my fill of Mr. Scrimm's delightful company, I had a chance to speak with my son, Miles. To listen to Miles talk down to me, to be more accurate. Him, with that Mormon wife and a whole warren of stinking children. How many mines do you suppose *he* has sunk into the Earth; what has he wrenched free from the rocks with his own hands? How many men has he employed? How much has he contributed to the economy of this whole damned *nation*?"

Cygnus drawls a reply as he drapes his lean body onto an overstuffed chair opposite Leonidas. "I don't imagine that he could lay claim to the plaudits due to you if that's what you're driving at. How *was* the reunion with your prodigal son?"

"He thinks that *I* am the prodigal. And he may be right. But that's not important— what is important is that he told me that he murdered Abner back in '48. Stabbed him through the heart and burned him to ashes."

This last statement by Leonidas causes Brimelow to lift his head and offer a rare interjection: "Did he *really*, now? Well, well. I may have misjudged your son, Mr. Pyburn. He's got some steel in him after all."

Leonidas ignores him. "We came for naught, Cygnus. Abner is dead, long dead and burned away. We have wasted our time."

"No, I do not think we have. As was *saying*, I arrived hereabouts yesterday, and I have made inquiries. Of Scrimm, certainly, but also of the night man who stands guard, and the sexton, and a few shovel-men besides Scrimm. He's a blind old goat, although I think he is blind by choice, and quite selectively. Whatever his excuse, there's no mistaking the signs and portents, nor the testimony of the men. They became nearly as chatty as Scrimm once their palms were crossed with silver. For which I kept no receipts, mind you, but I expect full compensation."

"And you shall have it, just as you always do." A flush has crept up Leonidas' neck and into his cheeks— a sure sign that he has neared the end of his temper. "Abner is dead."

"Something is sniffing after the graves at night, Frater Py-burn. Something feasts among the dead. The night man was so frightened by something he had seen that he babbled to me like a goose. He can't decide whether the thing he saw is an unusually bestial grave-robber or an unusually man-like beast, an eater of carrion." Cygnus turns his cane so that its silver head flashes in the light, a grinning corvid skull that complements his words. "I told him he was right on both counts and paid him to button his lip. For which, again, I kept no receipts. I regret my lack of proper bookkeeping; bribing illiterate workmen often proves a difficult matter when it comes to accountancy."

"Cygnus, you are not listening to me. Abner is *dead*."

"Oh yes," agrees the mage, "he is dead. I have no doubt of that. I saw as much myself, in my dream last night. I saw other things, too, Leonidas. Things of which you will want to hear. My Eye was busy."

Enough is enough, thinks Leonidas, and his patience with the baby-faced wizard is at an end. "*Charlatan!*" he bellows.

His explosion is loud enough that the china cup and saucer on his desk tremble, and Brimelow half-stands to attention, his focus suddenly on the scene unfolding before him. "I travel to this Territory of fundamentalists and idiots. I allow myself to be lectured by my son, who has decided to put his trust in an obvious lie and ridiculous fantasy. And all for *naught. Charlatan*, I say, and know this, Cygnus: I have had the occasional charlatan killed before when their deceit warranted it. I tell you no lie: I am not above stooping to *murder*, sir."

"No," murmurs Cygnus. "Nor to grave-robbing, it would seem."

This immediately takes the steam out of Leonidas. "*What?*"

"You deny it? You're wearing the goods as we speak, you brazen hypocrite, and you call *me* charlatan?" Cygnus' voice is quiet, even conversational, but there is no mistaking the sour bitterness in his tone. "I shall collect my things and be off, then. I suppose I shall expect no recompense for the funds I expended on your behalf. I should have expected no

171

better. A man does not become rich through noble thought or action, after all. I wish you the best in your endeavors, Mr. Pyburn, and take my leave."

"Wait," cries Leonidas. "Stay, Cygnus, and please forgive my outburst." Cygnus resumes his place on the overstuffed chair, though his posture remains stiff. "Tell me what you saw in your dream. Please."

Cygnus rises from his seat and takes a moment to nurse his wounded pride at the suite's bar, where he finds a tumbler and a bottle of halfway-decent whisky. He downs his first glass straight away, wipes his lips with a lace-edged handkerchief, and takes his time with his second tumbler, nursing the caramel-colored drink like mother's milk. Leonidas notes the provision of whisky in the suite with leaden cynicism. *Religious strictures*, he thinks, *are never as strict when large sums of money — and the men who represent those sums — are afoot. It's nice to know that even the Saints can, apparently, be bought.*

"It started," says Cygnus, "with you, Frater Pyburn. You, and a corpse, and a golden treasure, and a man you *thought* was dead."

Things click into place. "My God," Leonidas marvels.

"The one who survived his burial... I believe you said his name was Christiansen."

Chapter Nine

The Eye *is* Cygnus, and it is *not* Cygnus, both at the same time. It lives inside of him, inseparable, inescapable, indivisible, alien, and as cold as a scalpel's kiss. He can't remember a time before it was there, although when he *becomes* it— gives himself over to it and what it knows— he has a strange sense that the Eye is much older than he is, that its echoes stretch back into the cobwebbed past and forward into the shadowy half-truths of the future. He suspects that this feeling of connection to something eternal and ever-vast in its hunger is a byproduct of the Eye's ability to peek around the corners of existence as understood by mortal men. He becomes the Eye

174

by choice only occasionally. More often, the transfer happens by reflex, usually when he sleeps. Sometimes even while he is awake, darkness will claim him whole. In those moments, his sense of himself is pulled up and through something that feels like the neck of a bottle, but which, he supposes, must be his skull, the bony carapace tasked with keeping *in* what is, in this moment of terrible suction, suddenly *out*.

The journeys all begin the same way, with his newly separate capacity to *see* circling his body. The intelligence that fills his Eye is on some level alien, but it has been a part of him as long as his own thoughts. Its mental skin has always lain beside "his" own, and the limited autonomy given his Eye during these visions is a small price to pay for the view they have afforded him throughout the years. The view has been quite advantageous. Riches, men and women (and other folk besides) to warm his bed, warnings of plots laid against and harm intended to him— the spoils afforded him by his Eye have been constant and consistent. What he seeks, his Eye finds for him. There is a price, of course, as there is in all magicks, all natural processes from the chemical to the

175

physical, action and reaction. In his case, the price paid is the visions afforded him that he does *not* ask for, the ones that disturb his sleep with nightmares of places no human is meant to see, strange spaces and sideways times perpendicular to the flow of sense, terrible places that it hurts to think about. It is in no small part these surplus visions that have driven him to drink, to the opium pipe and philters, and just about everything else that can provide him pleasure or dull the clamor for a few moments.

Visions were easy— a Talent born to him. Sorcery, on the other hand— the physical manipulation of reality— came more slowly to Cygnus. The fact that he had to strive in his sorcery infuriated him into doubling and tripling his efforts until, in the end, his ability excelled beyond the aspiration of even the most naturally gifted mage. He read voraciously and sought out the obscure secrets known only by the outcast detritus of the world's underground occultists. Sometimes this was a literal description, as when he'd met a coven of warlocks in the catacombs beneath Paris. In spell-casting, the most valuable knowledge had all been hard-won. On the other hand, astral projection (as he eventually learned to call his journeys with his Eye) was second nature to Cygnus. It was one art in which he had never required instruction. Whatever methods of projection he did not find in his books came naturally to him, and his Eye had wandered far and wide until it had led him to Frater Pyburn, a fellow esoteric seeker with the riches of Croesus and a hunger for forbidden knowledge that rivalled Cygnus' own. Since the merger of their endeavors, his Eye had probed a great many dark places for Leonidas, and in recompense, Cygnus was given whatever he asked whenever he asked for it. To a man of Leonidas Pyburn's resources, the efforts required to secure Cygnus' loyalty were miniscule.

On the evening preceding his conversation with Leonidas, Cygnus had taken his usual nightcaps. His long-stemmed silver opium pipe was heating over its lamp, vaporizing the tarry substance in clouds of sweet, seductive smoke. Cygnus had complemented the experience with several glasses of hawthorn berry wine, sipped out of a port glass as he reclined on a couch in his own suite, more modest than the one selected by Leonidas but still nicer quarters than he has been accustomed to of late. His researches afford him less time in cities— even small, budding cities like Great Salt Lake City— than he would prefer, but as Leonidas would so crudely put his finger on the following night, it is the wind-scrubbed, sandy nowhere-places where Cygnus has acquired his most valuable artifacts. Places near gullies and mine shafts that swallow inconvenient corpses, places choked with dust that drinks blood, places ruled by corrupt or cowardly representatives of the law if such were to be found at all.

With the pipe's warm stem fitted to his mouth and the wine seasoning his blood, it's easy to ignore such thoughts, and that's what Cygnus had intended to do— until his Eye had asserted itself with mute ferocity. The feeling was more forceful than he was used to, his consent not requested or acknowledged. Once he has been pulled through his skull and into the Eye, floating free above his body, the sensation of a tremendous, directionless *pull* fills him, and the Eye is whisked away, over hill and dale, past frozen lakes and boiling hotpots, and, he becomes aware, back, back through the echoes of time, twenty years into the dead-and-gone.

Coming to rest for a moment, the Eye takes the measure of Leonidas Pyburn as he had looked decades before. Tired. Frightened half to death, but glad to be alive, glad his sons are safe (for so he still assumes). Not just younger, this Leonidas looks happier than he has ever looked in Cygnus' memory. *This is the face*, he thinks, *of a man I've never met. The version I know has been sorely corroded.*

Not that young Leonidas is an angel (or a Saint). As the Eye looks on, he manhandles a woman's corpse with fingers that linger too long on her breasts, fingers that squeeze and probe in a way that fills even the ice-cold Eye with disgust. Leonidas seems completely oblivious to the fact that he is observed by a spectral, temporally displaced presence as he adjusts his half-hard manhood, squeezing it with great affection as he rearranges his pants and shirttails to better obscure it. The Eye continues to watch as Leonidas spies a golden glimmer in the dirt and stoops to examine it. He turns the golden object with tender hands and brushes away the loose soil. He gives it a curious glance, then stuffs it into one of his pants' pockets. No matter. The Eye's gaze is incapable of cursory glances, and so it sees much in the few seconds it has to inspect Leonidas' treasure. He holds a heavy golden pendant on a fine gold chain, shaped like a peacock. The thing is a little bigger than a silver dollar. Cygnus' Eye sees how fine the craftsmanship of the peacock's feathers is— sees the cunning little jewels that have been wrought into the figure's eye sockets and the largest spots on its tail, and how the diamond chips scattered over its breast glitter in the gloom.

Leonidas returns to his work in the graveyard with his pocket weighed down with gold and precious stones. He does not tell either one of his sons what he found— *what he stole*, the Eye thinks with its cold and ruthless clarity.

¤

In the Delmonico, Cygnus pauses in his telling of the story: "You'll have to excuse me, Frater Pyburn, but this telling is thirsty work." He refills his tumbler with two fingers of whisky and gulps it down.

"Cygnus," says Leonidas, "I should have long since learned to shelve my skepticism where your visions are concerned, but this is profound even for you. Not one soul on Earth knows what you saw in your dream— besides me, I suppose."

"I regret to inform you that there is, in fact, *one* other soul who knows, though the soul in question may be so decomposed that it hardly retains any of its original human character. My dream continued after you and your sons left Winter Quarters to resume your journey west."

¤

The Eye has always seen more than just what transpires on the shiny surfaces of the world, and as Cygnus' dream continues, it peers into shadow and sees much.

In the darkness and silence of the void, dreamless and black as the space between the stars, a dim spark flares to life within Christiansen. Within him there is little of who— indeed, of *what*—he used to be; in its place, unfair though the trade be, there is hunger. Hunger that is both ravenous and specific. The thing that had been Christiansen struggles briefly against confinement, but he is weak, and the walls of the coffin feel as hard as iron, reinforced by the soil sur-

181

rounding them. Quickly, though, he loses interest in escape when he realizes his prison is not wholly bereft of benefits, for he has been locked in with a ready supply of meat in the form of his dead wife. Whatever is left of Christiansen the man violently rebels at the thought, but the hunger inside of him—the hunger that burns like fire in his warping bones and feverish, degraded brains— soon swamps that flame of aversion like an oily ocean quenching a candle. He feeds. And as he feeds, he changes and grows stronger.

Pulses and impulses reverse course inside of him; the circadian rhythms that served him as a man have been reversed and now serve him just as well. He senses the night when it comes and escapes, digging his way out of the coffin with newly long, newly strong fingers and muscles changed and driven by the malign new power source burning in his blood. Even with his chewed and diminished hand, he doesn't have much difficulty digging. His remaining digits are as hard as iron. Come nightfall of the following day, a day in which the three Pyburns continue their trek west and in which Abner continues to sicken, Christiansen slips free of the earth like a great, pale worm, his clothes shredded and stripped away by the coffin's ragged edges and the stony earth.

His refined senses drink in the rich buffet of decomposing meat around him, and without consciously doing so, he marks the cemetery as his scavenging grounds. He scuttles into the woods and finds what he's looking for: a stream, cool and clear. He drinks deeply, moaning with the relief of his thirst. Before dawn steals across Winter Quarters, Christiansen finds another thing that he requires: shelter. He makes his den in a small cave near the cemetery, nestled on the riverbank. He drives out a family of river otters without much difficulty. Like all animals, they sense something foul in him and flee his presence. The den suits him perfectly. It is snug, provides access to fresh water, and is remote enough to avoid discovery but within close proximity of his unspeakable pantry.

Perhaps Christiansen was possessed of a subtler mind in life than the thing that preceded him at the cemetery, or perhaps it had merely been as it was for so long that it had lost all its faculties. Whatever the explanation, he has managed to retain an edge of human cunning and craft that prevents him from making too much of a mess at the graves, sensing as he does that he shares the area with living men and women as well as the dead. The balance holds. The nearby living are few in number, his excavations are subtle, and his thefts from the bodies buried there only piecemeal. When he dines, he carries his treasures from the boneyard to his lair. Before long, his little cave by the river is cluttered with bones, all of them painstakingly cracked and sucked clean of both marrow and meat.

The Eye sees all of this, takes it in as condensed images that tell a story of years of half-life spent in darkness, years that, before long, become decades. Where Winter Quarters had been a squat little encampment on the Missouri River, Omaha now begins to rise. The land is carved up by claims, some more legitimate than others. Vigilante mobs, claim jumpers, and the dazzling assortment of criminals attracted by westward expansion all ensure a steady supply of corpses, many of them dumped directly in the river. This steady riparian stream of anonymous murders is a boon to Christiansen, as are the secret graves dug in the woods. His nose becomes attuned to the specific bouquet of human decomposition, and in time, he is able to sniff out these hidden bodies with ease.

So Christiansen lives, or exhibits something like a parody of life. By day, he sleeps. By night, he creeps up and down the river and feeds on the dead. Time passes, as time always does. The same process that gives Christiansen such strength and durability arrests the aging process. His remaining hair falls out; his eyes grow cloudy, and though he has trouble seeing in bright light, he can now see better in the dark than humans— his night vision is almost as advanced as that of the coyotes and other animals that slink by moonlight. This dark parade of death and decomposition is where he makes his home, where his un-life is now to be lived.

Until something… changes.

¤

"Hmmm. What changed?"

Cygnus' answer, at first, is the clink of crystal against glass as Cygnus makes himself another drink. Then the mage replies.

"As you know, what my Eye knows and what I can carry back to my physical body and waking mind are not, alas, the same. In my astral form, I knew *exactly* the stimulus that awakened new thoughts and feelings in our ghūl. When I awoke, I could only recall that it has to do with blood, and gold, and a family line— father-to-son, to be specific."

"Hmmm. But with Abner dead—"

"You produced *two* sons if I'm not mistaken. I do not know what role Miles has to play in this. In fact, I'm not certain that the father in question is you. Your son and firstborn grandson both may be required for the completion of our business here."

"That can be arranged, Frater Cygnus."

"I have nothing but confidence in your capacity in that regard, Frater Pyburn. This much I was able to bring from within the Eye: the task will require blood, and gold, and a son."

"So we collect Miles and young Lehi and set forth for Omaha without delay."

"That will not be necessary. As I learned from the grave-men at the City Cemetery, our ghūl is here already." And with another glass of whisky having washed the dust from his throat, Cygnus concludes his account of his dream and the things he had seen with the dark mirror of his Eye.

¤

The Eye rises like smoke into the sky over the settlement at Omaha, above the river and the red earth, and there it hov-ers like a minor sun. Below it, time compresses itself into a mad, insectile scurry. It watches as wooden structures rise and trees fall and roads are carved from mud and tall grass until thoroughfares blossom throughout the properties like veins in a leaf. And, at last, the railroad. It chews the land and leaves in its wake a long ribbon of steel that shines like a secret stream of molten moonlight.

One night, something in Christiansen shifts with a wrenching feeling, and he becomes achingly *aware* of the golden bauble Leonidas stole from his wife, his dear, de-voured wife. It lights up inside his thoughts like a beacon of fire; when he concentrates, he can even *see* Leonidas, dimly,

187

yes, but he can *see* him… And he is overcome with hate. In the dim recesses of Christiansen's brain, which has been, for the most part, swept away, the pull of his hate and his desire for the pendant set machinery in motion within him that by all appearances had decayed beyond recovery. Christiansen, while still retaining the feral disfigurement of his person-hood, begins to plan.

The train-yard is rarely silent, even in the middle of the night, but Christiansen has a stroke of luck one evening when the watchmen are otherwise engaged beating a tramp to a bloody pulp. He slips over the cinders of the yard as quickly and quietly as a plague-rat's shadow and takes shelter in a boxcar half-filled with empty burlap sacks. There, in the fur-thest, darkest corner of the car, Christiansen makes himself as small as he can and waits. Before long, the car rattles and shifts beneath him. The space is dark, and close, and dusty, but all things considered, it is nearly as cozy as his little cave by the river. As he waits, his hunger grows. A struggle begins between his reawakened capacity to think ahead and his im-mediate physical needs, but his self-control wins out, fueled by the frozen heat of his hate.

Bound for the West, the train travels through the blood-colored fire of sunset. As its last rays creep below the horizon, Christiansen reemerges from his makeshift burrow. In the warped recesses of his heart, a fierce joy springs into being and burns with an unfurling black flame. Christiansen cranes his body out of the train's car and lets the wind whip the few remaining strands of his hair like the long, ragged banners of a dead but conquering king. He gives his call, the one that has echoed through the boneyards of Omaha for untold years, into the rushing wind and darkness. His eyes are closed into ecstatic slits, and his wide-open mouth reveals the broken, bloody ruins of his teeth in a distorted grin. The Eye sees this from a fixed point above the train as it barrels along the plain, a black serpent with its own singular, blazing white eye.

The train arrives in Utah just before dawn. Christiansen knows—just as he can see Leonidas if he concentrates— that this is the place. He scuttles away from the train-yard and takes shelter from the coming daylight in a drainpipe that empties into the ditch near the yard's gravel perimeter. He is famished, but he sets his hunger aside and spends the day in a fitful doze in the half-darkness. At dusk, he awakes. Hunger has sharpened his already-keen senses even further, and he detects a scent to which he has become highly attuned coming from a farm about a mile from the yard. He has no trouble finding the handful of family grave plots, located at the far edge of the property. They're a recent addition, no older than a year or two. Christiansen probes them with his long, slender claws and drags forth the bodies of two small children. The banquet that follows is unspeakable. The Eye's frozen gaze spares Cygnus nothing.

Once he has fed, Christiansen follows the inscrutable pull of his instinct to the City Cemetery, near which he makes his new home. There, with the Eye watching, he digs a crude burrow beneath a thick stand of shrubs. At first, Cygnus' Eye is confused as to what the ghūl is doing. Then it is filled by a strange certainty: Christiansen has come here to wait for Leonidas. For the unfinished business of blood and gold.

¤

Leonidas clears his throat. His anger burns like a glowing, half-swallowed coal. "That boggart has been desecrating graves— eating *children*, for God's sake. And he has the brass to hate *me*? For what? Stopping when we should have pressed on? Helping an old man—at the price of my son's life!"

"Yes. No good deed goes unpunished, as they say." Cygnus' dream has been conveyed to Leonidas and the Eye sheathed (for now), and the mage now sounds a little drunk. "But though your son be gone, your intentions— our Great Work— they are not yet stymied. Now you have no need to convince Miles to leave his wife and children and warm little home to go chasing a ghost. May Abner rest in peace— but also let us acknowledge that there are advantages to this arrangement."

"Hmmm. I suppose so. We've been met halfway, and, as you said, this lessens the likelihood that force need be applied to Miles."

"In my conversations with the night man, as I said, he confirmed that there have been desecrations. He also told me about swirling rumors that the culprit was some local boogeyman— I think he was referring to a certain famous Italian Frenchman, the good Jean Baptiste. For a fortnight, the graves have been bedeviled. Which means that Christiansen has been here all that time. Waiting." Cygnus favors Leonidas with a vicious little smile.

"Waiting for *you*, Frater Pyburn. For you to be reunited with your family, and for you to bring him that which belonged to his wife, long since eaten and voided back into some noisome cave. And I can't help but wonder what he intends for *you*."

Part III

Great Salt Lake City (and Elsewhere)

Chapter Ten

"Hmmm. Did you know that this fair city has an entire street of ill repute? Oh, don't look so skeptical, Mr. Brimelow. After the Army tripped and fell into that vein of silver to the east of here, it was only a matter of time." Leonidas stares out of the window of the Delmonico, down onto a street lit by the eerie radiance of gas lamps where a quartet of drunks— two women and two men— stumble into one another and laugh riotously as they wind their way back to the hotel. Leonidas waves Brimelow to the window, and when the big man stands beside him, gestures down to the merry-mak-ers below. "The last of the night's revelers return home. Oh,

194

sin most foul, yes? But look there, at the corner—" Leonidas points. "That's Main Street, practically cheek-by-jowl with this fine establishment. There are so many saloons up and down its length that the citizens of Great Salt Lake City call it 'Whisky Street.'"

This draws a dry chuckle from Brimelow. "And there," Leonidas continues, "past 'Whiskey Street,' you can just see that low warren of rooms halfway down the block? That, sir, is 'Commercial Street,' and that is where those young gentlemen acquired their company for the evening. They are violating the unwritten laws of Great Salt Lake City, though, I'm afraid. As a rule, such activity is not to leave the confines of that most scandalous alley, let alone be carried on at the Hotel Delmonico."

"How come you to know all of this? You said you'd not been here before."

"And so I haven't— but you should know me better by now than to ask such a question, Mr. Brimelow. From the Knights of Labor to the Knights of St. Crispin, not so much as a proposed strike or the obvious superior pliability of

Chinese labor to Welshmen escapes my personal notice. Did you really think the city in which my son and grandchildren live would remain obscured to me?" Brimelow shrugs, and Leonidas sighs. "Well, Mr. Brimelow, I believe that should suffice for the day."

"I will stay tonight by your door."

"There's no need for melodrama. I think that the worst things this city can menace us with are its restaurants and the burning love its citizens have for the theater."

"Oh, I hate the theater," agrees Brimelow cheerfully. "All the same, I believe I will stay by your door."

"Suit yourself." Leonidas frees his swollen feet from his boots with difficulty, sighs, and slowly strips off the rest of his travel clothes, exchanging them for a long cotton night-shirt. He wears the golden peacock pendant against his bare skin, just as he always does, just as he has done every day since the struggle at Winter Quarters. He likes the feel of the gold against his naked flesh. He knows that others would say that it's all in his mind, but Leonidas thinks that he has a special relationship with gold. He'd had no particular genius before California, though he'd earned a decent living in a number of trades. He took to gold mining— or, rather, gold mine ownership— immediately, with a ferocity and single-minded purpose that grinds obstacles to dust, be they presented by nature, men, or laws. The feel of the gold against his skin calms him like the voice of a lover whispering sugar-sweet words. Something about its design had tickled his curiosity, and he'd performed his own researches into symbolism, though not as extensive as those conducted by his pet magician. The peacock was considered by the Greeks to be a symbol of immortality. They had believed that its flesh did not decay after death, and thus viewed it as representative of eternal life, the stasis of eternal continuation. Leonidas does not share this particular delusion, but the peacock *has* become his good luck charm, his totem, a thing that he had, in his mind, begun to think of as a symbol of his success, one that in his quieter hours he half-believed might even have some sort of supernatural quality. Cygnus had, after all, proved *his* strange talents again and again. With magic afoot in the world, it was not wise to dismiss anything out-of-hand. *That strange little man,* Leonidas thinks, and not for the first time. *If he is a man at all, that is. Can I trust him? Do I have a choice? Every year brings the grim specter of my mortal annihilation closer, inevitable second by unavoidable hour.* Well. If Christiansen had dragged himself halfway to hell to reclaim his dead wife's golden charm, was it so silly to think that the pendant might have some sort of special, even magickal, properties?

He douses the room's lamps, his preference being to read by candlelight in the evenings. His bed is too firm, the mattress unevenly stuffed and lumpish, but after the train and the cramped carriage, it feels heavenly to stretch his legs and recline on real pillows. Best of all, lying abed takes some of the strain off of his joints and affords him a bit of relief from his discomfort. Leonidas scans the room one more time. Brimelow could be a figure from a wax museum, motionless and obscured by the shadows near the door in his hard-backed chair. Leonidas attempts to struggle through a few more pages of Lévi's *Dogme et Rituel de la Haute Magie.* Halfway through a particularly dense passage on the Sabbatic Goat, he is dragged deep into sleep's bottomless black waters.

¤

In his dream, Leonidas stands at the foot of a great, steeply-sloping hill. Its crown is wreathed in mists of darkness, but through the swirling vapor, he can just make out a massive tree at the top, heavy with luminous white fruit. To one side of the hill's slope stands a great mansion, its many windows ablaze with golden light and the parapets and turrets of its heights just visible through the fog. Winding up the hill is a narrow path, the right-hand side of which is bounded by a long, ancient-looking iron rod which acts as a kind of bannister. Leonidas knows— as one knows in dreams— that the tree at the hill's peak bears the Fruit of Life, a prize he has sought in desperation for untold years.

Coiled at the base of the path, the very foot of the hill, is an enormous salamander. It is as white as snow save for its eyes, which shine and flicker with caustic, colorless flames. It regards Leonidas with contempt and, without warning, strikes him. It is a terrible blow and sends Leonidas sprawl-

199

ing to the dirt. When he regains his feet, the salamander has vanished. More cautious now, Leonidas places his hand on the iron rod as he mounts the path. The iron is pitted with corrosion and warm to the touch. As he climbs the steep path, Leonidas gazes over its edge to the sloping rock below him. At its lowest reaches, at the bottom of the slope, the land here sinks into a fetid bog, a place of roiling fog, grey, stagnant water, and a pockmark assortment of deep pits, all of them half-filled with a mud-and-quicksand slurry.

As he rounds a turn in the path, Leonidas is again confronted by the pale salamander. This time, it reclines in a shallow depression atop plates of gold that catch the dim and shifting light and shine with the luster that Leonidas has come to know so well. The moment he set his eyes on the plates, their glow intensifies, and they begin to melt as if cradled by a blazing fire rather than the salamander. The plates flow into each other, and, as though aided by an invisible sculptor, the molten gold hardens into a long, sharp object that Leonidas recognizes as a railroad spike. The salamander grips the spike and, this time, addresses Leonidas in a sweetly shifting voice, a voice of Water and of Gold, the same delicious tones that had first murmured to him in California, hunched with an aching back over a broad stream, gold pan in hand. "Seek you the pale fruit atop this hill?" asks the salamander. "And why? Why not the Fruit of the Knowledge of Good and Evil, which was proffered by my brother in the Garden?" Leonidas begins to reply but is again struck, again knocked to the dirt, and again, when he rises, the salamander is gone, and the spike with it.

Nearer now to the tree at the top of the hill, Leonidas presses on. As he passes nearer the great mansion with its blazing lights, Leonidas can see that all of its windows are crowded with grotesque faces that laugh and jeer and pour abuse upon him. Leonidas is enraged and ashamed, but despite his burning anger, he remains impotent. There is no visible way to reach the mansion, and even were he to do so, he has no interest in mansions or the company of those twisted, sneering faces. He himself owns more than one mansion, he dimly remembers from his waking life. His interest is in the fruit atop the hill, but more than that, what the fruit promises: life beyond death, beyond the reach of this cold and terrible place. Leonidas ignores the mansion and its occupants, though their barbs *do* sting.

At last, Leonidas reaches the end of the trail. His hand is still firm around the iron rod, his steps slow, sure, and steady. Suddenly, there it is: the tree, massive and ancient. Its roots must run the entire depth of the hill, Leonidas marvels, and its crown blots out the sky. Its branches are heavy with glowing white fruit, which looks delicious. The clusters of ripe fruit give off a pleasing scent than he can just detect from where he stands. He is unsurprised to see the white salamander this time, its body coiled around the tree's lowest branches. "And it came to pass," it says, its body drooping in loops of liquefying fire that erupt and evaporate, "that Leonidas met the angel and did wrestle with him." The fire falling from the tree coalesces, coagulates, and forms a flaming face of exquisite beauty, soon followed by a body, clad in blazing white, and two golden wings that spread behind it like the tail of a peacock. In fact, Leonidas notes, the angel's wings are bejeweled in a manner identical to Christiansen's peacock pendant. The angel speaks again, and this time its voice is thunder, its eyes twin rubies burning in a face of molten gold.

"Where is your son Abner?" it roars.

Leonidas is unmanned by terror and babbles in reply, "I don't know, am I responsible for my sons forever? Am I their *keeper*?"

"WHAT HAVE YOU DONE?" The angel's voice shakes the ground and freezes the marrow in Leonidas' bones. It is the voice of the Earth, the voice of Thunder, and it shakes him with a holy terror that he has never felt before in his life, dreaming or awake, a terror that breaks loose from the rational and becomes sublime. *"LISTEN! YOUR SON'S BLOOD CRIETH OUT FROM THE GROUND!"* Fire flashes, and in one hand, the angel now bears a great silver spear with a bladed tip. Just as the angel strikes with terrible force and speed, thrusting the spear through Leonidas' heart, the dreamer snaps awake, drenched in sweat and gasping.

¤

A mortal, bodily terror follows Leonidas from the dream

into the waking world, and he thrashes in bed, tangling himself with his bedclothes. Next to the door, Brimelow has left his chair, which lies all akimbo, toppled to the ground. His attention is fixed on the room's door, his big, meaty left hand wrapped around the handle of an enormous hunting knife. Leonidas has no need to speculate as to what has dragged him from sleep and raised Brimelow's alarm, because scant moments after he returns to consciousness, the night quakes with a long, desperate scream of terror, unmistakably female and coming from somewhere close by in the hotel. "In God's name, Brimelow, what was *that*?"

"Houl yer whisht," snarls Brimelow, brogue flaring like a fever, "and stay here." And with that, he slips out of the suite and closes the door behind him. Leonidas has no intention of following Brimelow's admonishment and works himself out of the tangle of bedclothes after a few seconds of struggle. At the bottom of a leather valise near the bed is a derringer pistol. Leonidas checks that it's loaded and secrets it into one palm. He dons his robe and slippers and follows after Brimelow into the hallway of the Delmonico's top floor.

Waiting for Leonidas in the hallway is a scene of terror. The scream that had awakened him and had so alarmed Brimelow came from one of the ladies of the evening who had made her drunken way to the hotel earlier that night in the company of a female companion and two well-heeled men (who were, as it would turn out, would-be silver barons, recently enriched, though hardly sojourners in the same galaxy of wealth and power in which Leonidas conducts *his* affairs). The women, having seen to affairs of their own, ones which the silver barons *were* privy to, had just left the barons' suite on the top floor. Through screams and babbling from the survivors, Leonidas can just make out what had apparently happened next. In the hallway, the courtesans had startled something or someone— whether it was, in fact, a wild animal or a crazed, naked bandit was unclear. The misshapen thing had torn out the throat of one of the women. It was her companion who had screamed. The victim is quite incapable of giving voice to such herself as she expires, her blood drenching the Delmonico's carpets. The thing— whatever it was— having dealt the woman a mortal injury, fled by way of the same window through which it had gained access to the third floor of the Delmonico. The hotel's exterior, while composed of windows and smooth wood, was hardly sheer, and it had managed to scuttle down the side of the hotel and into the night before any other witness could get a clear look at it.

The walls and floor of the hallway are painted in great, bright-red fans of blood. So much of it has pulsed from the dying woman that there's a coppery stink that hangs in the air like perfume. Leonidas has personally seen enough blood spilled over his years settling disputes in the mines that he has proven himself anything but squeamish when it comes to a little judicious shedding of the stuff when necessary. He and Brimelow are not in the middle of nowhere at a mining camp, nor in a bare-bones town where lawlessness and murder are an unremarkable, even integral, feature of the landscape. Great Salt Lake City seems a place half Saint, half sinner, but with both camps engaged in an uneasy and mutually beneficial détente. *The holocaust of blood in this hallway*, Leonidas thinks, *would be but one of many nightly brutalities in*

206

a mining camp. Here, there is sure to be an uproar— and there's even a damned eye-witness.

Brimelow, without missing a beat, turns and buries his knife in the screaming woman's throat and twists. Immediately, her cries are severed with a croak, and the torrent of her lifeblood pours forth. She stares, eyes agog, at Brimelow. Her face is, Leonidas observes, a very amusing portrait of shocked surprise, if one can ignore the spastic working of her jaw as blood spills from it and joins the torrent that rushes from her throat and soaks her dress. With a movement as quick and as fluid as the one with which he buried the knife in her flesh, Brimelow rips it free, wipes it clean on the inside lining of his coat, and returns it to his sheath. All of this is carried out in scant moments. From the quick and practiced stealth of the maneuver, it's apparent that Brimelow is accomplished at the art of surreptitious execution. He accomplishes his bloody work with nary a second to spare: the woman's screams have drawn one of the silver barons from his suite, as well as a bellhop from downstairs. Both would-be witnesses arrive too late to hear the woman's babbled words or catch Brimelow at his grim work.

"Merciful *God*," cries the silver baron as he stumbles onto the scene. His tongue is thick with liquor and horror. "Merciful *God*, but... but... what *happened*?"

The change that overtakes Brimelow's effect is remarkable. His lips tremble, his eyes grow as wide as twin moons, and his hands shake. "Oh, saints *preserve* us! A young man— dressed in rags, with a mad look in his eye— he had a *knife*—" In the pandemonium that erupts, Brimelow and Leonidas return to the suite with scant attention paid to them.

"Mister Brimelow," Leonidas says as the door closes behind them. "I am not sure which is more impressive— your improvisation when it comes to the speedy dispatch of troublesome persons or your unexpected skills as a thespian."

Brimelow shrugs his big shoulders but allows himself a half-smile. "Was it Christiansen?"

"Aye," says Brimelow. "He looks worse than what you or Mr. Cygnus described. And sweet *Jesus*, Mr. Pyburn, the *smell* of him. There's very little of the man left in that thing, I'd warrant."

"After twenty-two years of living in a cave, defecating where he sleeps, and feeding on the ripe meat of human carcasses, I cannot say that you or I would be in any better condition."

In the hallway, a riotous chaos of voices rises, one shouting over another. The civil authorities have, it seems, finally arrived on the scene. Whatever hot words are being exchanged are too muffled by the suite's door to be deciphered. "Mister Brimelow," Leonidas says. He dresses with slow, careful movements, joints as stiff as ever. "I feel it would be in our interest to accelerate our timetable a bit."

"Yes, sir."

Brimelow departs into the bedlam in the hallway, and Leonidas checks his gear. Two revolvers this time. A heavy canvas over-shirt and canvas gloves. The shirt's collar is fortified with steel plates that cover the neck and throat, and the gloves are similarly reinforced. Lanterns. Rope. Nets. A long pole with a slip-noose dangling from one end. All seems in readiness. He has ample time to double- and triple-check these requisitions before there's a quiet knock at the door;

Brimelow has returned.

"Miles seemed reluctant to leave his bed at this hour," Brimelow says.

"Slothful. That sounds like him." Leonidas, geared up for the evening's excursion, looks a little bit like some ridiculous subclass of knight, one with canvas armor and a loop-ended lance. "I trust that you did not accept his excuses?"

"They are in the carriage downstairs. I made it clear that it would be most unwise for them to leave its confines while I've been collecting you." Brimelow glowers under the bill of his cap. "That lot in the hall were the real heavy lift, but I managed, with the help of no small amount of your coin."

"Good man," says Leonidas. "Well. We'd best be off, then, haven't we?"

Chapter Eleven

Leonidas has come to understand that midnight is only thought to be the "witching hour" by those with little to no experience with the rhythms of the night. The long, bleak hour between two and three in the morning has always been the stretch of time in which deeds are best carried out that would shock and horrify the sunlit world. This has held true in both London and the wilds of the Dakota Territory and is no less true in the City of Great Salt Lake. The handful of gas lights that dot downtown spread their pale glow over streets bereft of people and storefronts shut tight and dark against the night. Overhead, the moon is small and very bright, adding its own cold illumination to the play of shadows as Leonidas and Brimelow exit the Delmonico and find their coach— its driver well-paid to rouse himself and ferry them at this hour —and its occupants waiting. Brimelow, a head taller than Leonidas and half again as wide, has to fold himself to squeeze in alongside their guests.

On one side of the coach sit Brimelow and Leonidas; squeezed into the other are Cygnus, Miles, and Lehi. Miles is livid. "Whatever this is, father, it can wait until morning. For decency's sake, if nothing else. This is *ridiculous*." Miles begins to get to his feet, and Leonidas nods at Brimelow, who delivers a compact, vicious blow to Miles' solar plexus. Though the quarters are close, Brimelow is experienced at delivering such pain, and Miles falls back into his seat like a boned fish, his wind gone. A look of bright terror fills Miles' and Lehi's eyes.

"Hmmm. It *cannot* wait, actually." Leonidas bangs on the roof of the carriage, and it rolls away from the Delmonico. Five persons are a full load, and the cab's springs sag and complain. With every bounce and jostle of their journey,

Brimelow and Leonidas (who is, himself, not a small man) crowd each other.

"I see," says Leonidas, "that Mr. Brimelow's argumentation has left you speechless. That's a state I would encourage you to maintain until spoken to, Miles. Worry not, I will keep this as brief as possible. First, a word about your book and its entry on the ghūl: it was, for the most part, accurate, if a little coarsened and scrambled by translation. But your book was not the first time I encountered a description of the species.

"Frater Cygnus here, of course, knew of them well before I did, which is not surprising. Hmmm. His knowledge exceeds, I will admit, the amount that I am likely to accumulate in this life, however long I live. He first encountered them in Cairo, a city replete with poorly-guarded corpses and full of ancient superstition, both conditions being highly favorable to the ghūl. The development that most excites me took place well outside of what passes for modernity in Egypt, however, in Giza. Cygnus was part of an expedition charged with recovering certain items from an obscure tomb, the location of which had become available thanks to his talents. The par-

213

ty found what they were looking for, at the expense of a few of their number to banditry, and the artifacts were retrieved from their resting place. The most important discovery, however, had nothing to do with magick baubles.

"You see, the arrangement the good Frater's employers made with local grave-robbers emphasized that the mystical items that Cygnus' client required were only a few in number. The rest of the tomb's contents, the employer had assured them, were theirs to keep as payment. This turned out to be a remarkably generous offer, as the tomb was a trove of gold and priceless artifacts, enough for any man to live like a king for the rest of his days. But greed is a funny thing, isn't it? When men get the taste of gold in their mouths, they acquire an unquenchable thirst for it— and often for blood, as well. I know this better, it could be argued, than any other man alive on Earth. I've profited handsomely by men's taste for gold. Built an empire, really, on the simple truth of greed. Greed and power, Miles: *that* is the world, and all of your church fathers' pretty lies won't change things one jot or tittle."

"Father," says Miles, "what *happened* to you in California?"

Leonidas ignores this. "In this case, too, one man's greedy undoing was the impetus for my gain. The grave robbers were driven half-mad by the sight of all the gold that lay in that tomb, and they resolved not to leave so much as one *geneih* behind. In their thoroughness, they uncovered the entrance to a secondary tomb that lay below the first. When they unsealed it, they found a *ghul*.

"Now, what I'm about to tell you is remarkable, almost unbelievable, but based on the archaeological evidence, it cannot be disputed that this creature had been sealed up in that chamber, alive, for *millennia*. It had no food source, having consumed whatever nourishment may have been interred with it ages ago. The chamber was air- and watertight, so the thing had continued to exist without breathing or drinking. It had entered a state of hibernation of some kind, and our men mistook it for one of the withered mummies that populate the necropolis. Before they understood what was transpiring, it awoke and killed two of them. The survivors rallied and gave chase. The creature was disoriented—not surprising given its long somnolence—and they pursued it out of the tomb, into the sunlight. The moment the sun touched its flesh, it began to smolder and squeal, and the light struck it stone dead within moments. Its flesh melted like rancid butter in the sunlight, leaving naught more than bones and gristle within an hour."

"Riveting. You tell the story almost as if you were there," Cygnus drawls. His voice is as dry and sweet as vermouth.

Leonidas ignores this, too. "When I began my own researches into this subject, Frater Cygnus' name was mentioned more than once. He and I are both members of an Order given to esotericism and direct experience with the occult sciences. Our paths to this fellowship of true knowledge began within a society dedicated to helping the widow's son. Soon, though, we found the strictures of that group too confining. The project we soon swore to pursue together required a certain... *flexibility* that they lacked." Cygnus smiles at this.

"What, exactly, is this 'project?'" asks Miles.

"Immortality," Leonidas says simply. Miles and Lehi look deeply uncomfortable at this.

"Father," Miles says warningly, "we're venturing dangerously close to the red-hot shores of blasphemy against Almighty God, and that is a thing I am afraid I cannot conscience."

"Stow your pious nonsense, boy," snaps Leonidas. "Do you think I'm talking about my *soul*? No, no, sir. I will leave the 'soul' as the province of mystics and charlatans. It's the immutability of the flesh that I seek, nothing less, nothing more."

"Father." Miles' tone is as careful as if he were handling a wasp's nest. "There is one way and one way alone to secure that, and it is to repent of your sins and abide in the Lord."

"You are incorrect in that," says Leonidas. "But it doesn't matter. You may abide in your Lord, if you wish, and as you crouch, naked, filthy, and miserable in the rotting manse of that decrepit deity, I, unfettered by such excremental superstition, shall—"

Somewhere within the soft exterior gifted to him by a

217

stable family life hides the boxer Miles had been—the bare-knuckle fighter, the man who scrapped in bars and laughed while he bled. This Miles has been hiding, and Leonidas' words summon him forth. He delivers a single straight left to his father's chin before the big bodyguard can so much as register the shift in Miles' shoulders. It's a beautifully de-livered punch, crisp and accurate and executed without an ounce of wasted energy. Leonidas' head snaps backward on his neck and collides with the interior of the cab with a hol-low *THWOCK!*

"*Damned bugger!*" roars Brimelow, lunging for him.

"Mister Brimelow, no!" Leonidas barks, and Brimelow releases Miles' neck where he had seized it.

"Hmmm." The elder Pyburn rubs his chin with a rueful grin. "Now, I had wondered where my son was, whether he was still there inside of this…" He gestures at Miles. "*Mormon choirboy* I've been dealing with. Nice to see you again, Miles. It took a distressing amount of time for you to stop showing me your belly and show me your teeth instead."

A flush creeps up from the edge of Miles' collar. He ignores Leonidas, but when he turns his bright blue eyes to Lehi, Leonidas can see them dance with an excitement kindled by the thrill of combat, however short or aborted it was, and however illicit the pleasure might be. "Do not be like me, Lehi. Most especially, do not be like your grandfather. There is no small part of the Devil in me, and though we pray for the old man, his soul is as black as boot polish. And he is too old, too mean, and too rich to change his ways now."

"Allow me," Leonidas replies, "to offer young Lehi some advice of my own. Do not be like this version of your father. He used to have gumption, a pint of vinegar in him. He used to have *balls*, boy. He was a laugher and a brawler. This neutered version mewling before me is a travesty. An abomination." He clears his throat. A flush has crept up from his own collar, and a vein pulses in Leonidas' broad forehead. "Try to keep your balls if you can, Lehi, though the world may try to clip them. If you preserve your manhood, it may carry you out of this valley of the damned Saints one day. Perhaps you've even got enough Pyburn blood in you for me to take you on as an office-boy or find you employment in an administrative capacity at one of the mines."

"As God as my witness, Leonidas Pyburn," says Miles, "I shall see you dead and buried before I see my son anywhere near your fetid little empire."

"Oh, it's not so little these days." Leonidas glowers out his window at the night, washed in cold and distant moonlight. They are the only carriage on the streets, indeed, the only people who seem to be about at all. "And *kill* me, boy? Others have tried, men with means and cunning. Better men than you. Forgive me if I fail to tremble at the awesome power of your threat." Lehi, for his part, remains stock-still and silent. His eyes are as wide as two fish-ponds in which his pupils swim, panicked, between darting glances at Leonidas and at Brimelow.

"Father." Miles' tone is placating, reasonable— a man trying to talk sense into someone who has temporarily taken leave of their wits. "We are *no part* of this. Whatever it is that you think you're doing here, if I cannot persuade you to turn aside your course— and I do beg you to do so— at the very least, leave me and my boy out of it. Look, we are almost back on Wall Street. Let us depart here, and we'll walk away, and we can be shed of each other. Or, in Heavenly Father's name, at least let Lehi go. With all your money and the men at your disposal, what could you possibly need with him?"

"I think I have explained quite enough, Miles. Now shut your idiot mouth, if you please. We're already here." And, indeed, the carriage rolls to a stop at the very edge of the City Cemetery. The only illumination comes from the cold remoteness of the moon. The air is bitter cold but sweet on the tongue. The Cemetery, like all green places, breathes at night, an exhalation of dew-damp grass, healthy trees, and the subtle perfume of the black earth displaced to sink coffins into their long, dark, subterranean slumbers. Brimelow is the first to exit the cab, and he helps Leonidas descend after him. The elder Pyburn's joints are as stiff as rusted hinges this night; his descent is difficult. By the time all five passengers have been decanted, the squash-faced driver is already asleep, muttering deep into his woolen layers.

¤

They walk single-file in deep shadows and exchange not

221

a word as they press deep into the Cemetery. Cygnus leads the way. He carries a small object swaddled in stained burlap under one arm and is shrouded almost completely by a black hooded cloak with its cowl pulled back. The spray of his blonde ringlets looks white against the dark fabric in the moonlight; he is an eerie sight and looks every inch the magician. Behind him are Lehi and Miles. Their steps are uncertain but aided from time to time by a firm push from Brimelow, right behind them. He bears a satchel that contains Leonidas' various preparations for the evening: the pistols, the reinforced garments, all slung on the long body of the dog-catcher's pole. Last in line, Leonidas' stiff gait leaves him trailing the other members of the group by a half-dozen paces.

At first, Miles thinks that they have interrupted either a surreptitious burial or a desecration in progress— but no, the two figures that swim out of the darkness as they reach the heart of the Cemetery are not engaged in grave-digging, nor grave-robbing. They wait, in fact, for Cygnus and the others. They stand just beyond a ring of four freshly-dug graves, each with a shovel stabbed deep into its surface. The wooden handles of the shovels have been cocooned in burlap tied in place with wire; they stand like four pillars bereft of an awning. In their center stand three simple wooden chairs. Miles is not sure why, but the sight of the chairs sitting vacant among the fresh graves in the Cemetery under the impassive light of the moon… It fills him with dread. *Perhaps,* he thinks, this is *the still, small voice I am so often reminded to listen for?*

Cygnus withdraws the object under his arm from its sack, revealing a diminutive lantern. At his touch, it springs to luminosity, casting a weird pinkish light. It does not flicker, nor does it glow steadily. Rather, it throbs with light like the beating of a heart. The pink glow's intermittent brightness strikes four angular penumbra from the shovel-handles. The spidery shadows disappear, then reappear, then disappear again with the flux of the light. In his black cloak with his ebony walking-stick, face illuminated from below by the pulsing light, and eyes gleaming with savage good humor, Cygnus looks— Miles thinks— unnatural. *Father said he sought immortality,* thinks Miles. *Is it possible that he has, in his ignorance and atheism, struck a deal with an agent of Satan? This "Cygnus" certainly looks the part.*

The two figures waiting for them could be taken for fallen creatures of the Pit, he supposes. One is an Indian woman. Her face bears terrible scars that twist the lid of one eye and pull at the corner of her mouth. Her black hair is pulled back, and she is clad from neck to feet in soft leather, a patchwork of skins and furs. She appraises the quintet of men with deep black eyes, nonplussed. The other figure resolves itself in the throbbing light and reveals a skinny, twitchy man with a loathsome little moustache. The suit he wears is clean but threadbare and might have been quite fashionable a decade earlier. Strapped to his scrawny hips are two enormous revolvers in low-slung holsters.

Cygnus' voice has lost all of its weightless mirth and is as cold and flat as a snake's gaze as he speaks up. "We've assembled the constituent components, Mr. Pyburn. All of them except for our guest of honor, that is, but I suspect we'll have to wait just a bit longer for him."

"Hmmm. Very well." Leonidas makes his way to the

chairs, pulls one around to face the other two, and sits with effort. "Come on over here, boys, and make yourselves comfortable. You heard Frater Cygnus; we could have a wait ahead of us."

"I will give you one more chance," Miles says. "Just let us walk away, father."

"I believe I've had just about enough of your lip for one night. For one lifetime, really." Leonidas nods at Brimelow, who strikes from behind and hikes one boot upwards into Miles' testicles. Miles falls to the ground as though his guts have been set on fire, which is, indeed, what the pain is like. "Have a god damned seat, Miles," Leonidas says, patting one chair in front of him. During this exchange, Lehi has balled his fists and braced himself to fly at Brimelow, but Miles grabs hold of him with one hand.

"*Don't*, Lehi," he gasps, and with his son's help, struggles to his feet. Leonidas watches this with a mixture of dull amusement and patience. Gingerly, painfully, Miles takes a seat, and Lehi sits beside him.

"I purchased the services of our two friends here," Leonidas says, "because they both have experience with the type of bloody madness that we are likely to have on our hands this evening. Left Hand over there—the squaw with the scars? She has killed a dozen of those foul things, not to mention her other run-ins with the lesser-known wildlife of the West. You've become a bit of an authority on monsters, haven't you, Left Hand?"

"Monsters," she says. Her eyes are utterly penetrating as she stares at Leonidas, up and down, and her voice is all barbed wire and bad memories. "Yes."

"Hmmm. And Joe Peck, I think, is the name you gave us? Joe's skills are a bit broader and less particular in nature. No specialist. But renowned for the bottomless depths of your discretion nonetheless, aren't you, Joe?"

"Hah?" Peck's face is dark with grime, and the powerful smell of a distillery's worth of whisky wafts off of him. "Oh! Be assured, s'just between us. It was twenny-five, folding cash, after we're done, yuh?"

"Splendid," says Leonidas drily. "Well then, I suppose we have space in which to breathe for a second. If either of you pious men wishes to make his peace with God, this will most likely prove your last opportunity, so take advantage of it if you wish your consciences cleansed."

"Lehi and I have no need to be shriven. We stand ready to pass beyond this world. We are not perfect, but we have led lives devoted to a higher cause than the material, a more pure Divinity than anything offered by greed or power. Should we die here, tonight, we die *clean* and can thus face anything the next worlds may present to us, unafraid and full of love. Can you say the same?"

To this question, Leonidas has no ready reply.

Chapter Twelve

The dull pink illumination of Cygnus' lamp lends the illusion of movement to the tombstones that sporadically dot the dark landscape surrounding the little group. Though the stones do not move, the procession and recession of their shadows produces the illusion that they hunch and hover, breathing like silent golems, observers to the party's cemetery congress. Joe Peck wanders the perimeter of their circle, always in nervous motion, hands never far from the butts of his guns. Left Hand, seated comfortably atop one of the grave markers, watches him pace and mutter with her black eyes. An expression plays about her scarred lips that might

228

be amusement or a species of distant contempt. Brimelow, as always, has not left Leonidas' side and stands directly behind him, one hand clasped around the long wooden handle of the dog-catcher's pole.

Into this uncomfortable silence Leonidas lobs a bomb. "I suppose in all this excitement you think it has escaped me somehow that you've confessed to me to the murder of your brother, my youngest boy. It has not."

"Murder? I did not *murder* Abner! What I did was a mercy. Have I spent wakeful hours turning it over in my mind, pondering if there was another way to save him? Of course I have. When we decided to leave him in that pit— and yes, we *decided*, father— we damned him. All I did was offer him the first step toward redemption. Toward eternal progression."

"When you say that word, 'redemption,'" says Leonidas, "I feel ashamed that I fathered such a sickening fool."

"You feel sick because you *are* sick. But your words have lost the ability to wound me. I may have killed Abner, but I also saved him. Saved him *twice*, in fact. Once when I ended his unnatural corruption and burned his defiled flesh.

And then a second time the only way I could. I saved him by proxy baptism."

"Mr. Brimelow, is this mewling zealot trying to tell me that he baptized my son… *after* his death… into this loathsome polygamist cult? Thus heaping even *further* humiliation upon what was already a shameful end?"

"I believe he is." Brimelow's face is impossible to read in the deep shadows of his cap, but his voice is laced with both contempt and a dangerous, dancing amusement. "Shameful thing that would be, Mr. Pyburn. Not unlike grave-robbing, in truth."

Cygnus, perhaps feeling protective of his fellow grave-robber, speaks up. "Though Smith's charlatanism and lustful habits are well-established, he was not without some of the Talent, and he had such a respect for certain tenets of my Order that I cannot help but feel reciprocal affection for the man. In truth, of the Protestant Christianities, the Saints are closest to the real meat of the thing in some regards, and their Prophet was even wise enough to liberally salt his faith with magicks."

"How *dare* you, sir," barks Miles. "'*Magicks*?' We hold the keys of the Priesthood and the power of the restored Church of Jesus Christ. We have no truck with devils, whose sulfurous stink fairly surrounds *you* in a damnable nimbus."

"Is that so, Priest of Melchizedek?" At this, Miles stiffens. He struggles to keep the surprise from his face and fails. "How do you… How *could* you…" he trails off.

"Oh, very little on this Earth— or any other— is *truly* hidden from those who know how to look and have a mind to. And nothing whatsoever is hidden from my Eye. Would you care to hear how it all ends for you, who have been anointed a King and a Priest in the exaltation that is allegedly to come?"

To this point, Lehi has been silent. Now, when he speaks up, he trembles a bit at first, but his voice is as clear as a hammer-struck silver bell. "'And it came to pass that there were sorceries, and witchcrafts, and magicks; and the power of the evil one was wrought upon all the face of the land, even unto the fulfilling of all the words of Abinadi, and also Samuel the Lamanite.' Mormon 1:19." He looks at the magician, and the verse seems to have bolstered his resolve. For the first time since Brimelow collected them in the middle of the night, there isn't a trace of fear in Lehi's face. He has his father's bright blue eyes. They regard the magus the way an intelligent raven might inspect a turtle, looking for a way into its armor. The smile that Cygnus offers in return is dead, and cold, and very wide. In the unnatural light of his lantern with his eyes crinkled in joyless mirth, the sorcerer could be twenty years old or two hundred.

"'The evil one,'" he mocks. "It's always the same with you Abrahamics."

Left Hand, not by nature loquacious, interjects from her seat atop the gravestone: "Whatever you have had trade with, wizard, it is an unclean power. I do not worship the Cannibal God. I do not think I have any god at all. Regardless of that, I, too, smell evil upon you."

"All these scandalous lies, these assertions that I reek of brimstone. I'm hurt. I spend enough at the parfumerie that I assure you such a thing is simply not possible. If anything, I smell of sandalwood." The night air reverberates with a loud crunching sound that causes Lehi to wince.

Brimelow has brought an apple, which he continues to ostentatiously enjoy as Leonidas says, "I have always found your bouquet delightful, Frater Cygnus." He turns to Left Hand. "You seem unusually chatty. Why don't you go help Joe Peck keep watch?" Left Hand shrugs and ambles away, hands in her pockets. "You know," says Leonidas, "Mr. Brimelow, Cygnus, perhaps I do not appreciate your professionalism enough. In contrast to the quality of person I have had to deal with in this Territory, you men shine like diamonds." He turns to Cygnus. "Are we in readiness?"

"Assuredly. Consider the bond of blood and the stolen gold, the symbol of eternal life— yes, I believe this arrangement ought to do the trick. Take the pendant out from beneath your shirt. Wear it in the open where he will be able to smell it." Leonidas does as he is instructed. Even in the moonlight, the gold peacock shines with a beautiful, muted luster, soft against the canvas of Leonidas' reinforced canvas overshirt.

"Where *who* will be able to see it?" Miles tries to slow

the hammering of his heart, to will his fluttering stomach to settle down.

"Someone we thought dead and buried. Back at Winter Quarters, if you can believe it. They're calling the place Omaha these days."

"*Christiansen*?" Miles shakes his head. "That's impossible. He's naught but bones by now, twenty years in the ground."

"I had the same reaction when first I heard the tale. But Frater Cygnus has convinced me that our long-last compatriot has for a fortnight now been sniffing about this very graveyard— that, indeed, we will be graced with his presence soon enough. And won't *that* be a tender reunion, eh, Miles? Let's hope you show a few more yards of guts tonight than you did back then, hmmm? Or do you plan to sacrifice your boy upon the same bloody altar of cowardice on whose stony breast you murdered your only brother?" The savagery of Leonidas' words stands in contrast to the expression on his face which displays, if Miles had to nail the expression down in one word, boredom.

"Was it the gold that made you this way? Or have you

always been this man? Was the man who dandled me on his knee and let me pull his moustache, who stayed up all night long by Abner's bedside when he was almost taken from us by influenza, was he just a mask? Has this *hate* been inside of you all along?"

The appearance of boredom notwithstanding, these words fly far and strike Leonidas deeply. "It was supposed to be the *three* of us Miles, can't you understand that? Two loyal sons and a father, three men who would shape the future, who would make their fortunes. I was going to start a dynasty," he says. "The Pyburn name was to stand like Vanderbilt. We were to build vast estates, and generations of our descendants would have been American royalty. Instead, you murdered your brother in his filth and shame, and now even *you* live on a cloud born of religious fantasy. You, too, are lost to me— lost to the real world. All because of Christiansen. *Think* of what he took from us, Miles. Well, I aim to take something back. Immortality by other means, if my original dream is to be denied me."

"You wish to be translated," says young Lehi. "Like the

Three Nephites. But that is reserved for a very especial few, grandfather. You *can* have exaltation, if you work toward it in this life and beyond. It is not too late to experience the resurrection, to gain your celestial body and live forever, just as you wish."

Brimelow tosses his apple core to the ground and swallows the last of its flesh. "Lehi, you seem a bright enough lad. You remind me of my nephew. Just like him, you are a sweet boy. You have that sweetness in you because, to this point, you have been blissfully unacquainted with suffering. I don't wish to be the man who changes that for you, but have no doubt that I will be that man, should you not shut up your mouth and keep it shut." From the big Irishman, this is a veritable monologue.

Lehi does not need to be told again. In both the rough-and-tumble world of adolescent boys in the Salt Lake valley and the rigid but depthless love of the ward, Lehi has been expertly tutored in the eternal, brutal lessons of hierarchy. Certainly, the hierarchy of adult men over boys, in particular. Recently, too, he was initiated into the mysteries of the

Aaronic Priesthood, a bond with his father that he alone of his brothers and sisters can claim. Perhaps most importantly: despite Leonidas' scorn and Brimelow's condescension, Lehi is not a naïf. He has grown up west of (most) war, but also west of the laws that govern gentiles. At some level, he— like all the boys he knows— has had to reconcile his religious principles with the frontier realities of human cruelty and the human willingness to inflict pain.

Perhaps the Earth is Hell after all, Lehi thinks, *and we are the devils who make of it a brutalism, a crime against the love that Heavenly Father has for all men. It is, after all, but one incarnated step along our plan of salvation.* While the theological flowers and hopeful coda of this thought will die with time, stripped away by withering contact with the vicissitudes of the real world, its bedrock— *we have made our Hell on Earth*—will remain with him from this moment until the end of his days.

It is the first hard lesson that he learns from Brimelow, but it is far from the last.

¤

A few yards from the Pyburns, at the edge of the throbbing light cast by Cygnus' lantern, Left Hand circles the camp in a leftward direction— "widdershins," as her friend back in Laramie calls it. *Called* it, she corrects herself, and the thought is still bitter after two years. Burned as a witch: she had heard tell of such things in the East, centuries removed, but evidently, the children of the Cannibal God's thirst for witch-blood remains unslaked. She is all too aware of the risks posed by her choice of vocation, the prey she pursues and her penchant for raising the ire of priests of the Cannibal God. Her longevity thus far has been a product of her ruthlessness, yes, but more than that, of her superb perception and clear-headedness. These last two qualities are sorely lacking in the person of Joe Peck.

"I don' like it," he mumbles, squinting into the night beyond the carmine glow of their little circle. He walks beside her and only sways on his feet every three or four steps. His hands, Left Hand notes, are shaking like leaves above his scuffed gun-butts. "Cemetery at night. Some damned warlock. And the ol' man— he plays it like a fancy one, but I think he likes th' taste of blood." *Fair enough*, thinks Left

Hand, *maybe he is not as stupid as he seems*. She says nothing.

Joe Peck managed, somehow, to secret a flat glass pint of whisky within his suit coat, which he now retrieves. He is as scrawny as a string bean, the suit a bit tight and very shoddy— Left Hand is curious where he managed to hide the pint. He drinks deeply from it and proffers the bottle to Left Hand. She shakes her head, and he mutters, "Suit y'self," takes another slug, and slips the pint back into the mysterious inside pocket of his coat. Joe's tongue darts between his lips; it surfaces, a pink, greasy flash chasing the phantom sweetness of whisky, and then it vanishes once more. "Lemme tell you a tale, about the country out here. By those scars, I'd warrant that you know its nature— still, worth hearin' me out. Was a while back, couldn't tell you how long, exactly. I was down in Arizona Territory. They had some trouble with th' Yavapai, out Prescott and Agua Fria way, and was looking for volunteers. Pay was pretty good, too, so I joined up, and we rode out. One night later, I was the only one alive—but it weren't the Yavapai that did for us.

"We made camp in the desert. I don't know what it was

woke me up, but when I came to, *they* were in the camp. They had faces like men and women, but they was so *tall*, and dressed in black from neck to the ground, gloves and all. They was bent over the bedrolls of some of the men. It was an unnatural thing to see, right? So I yelled and let off a shot, and damned if they hadn't disappeared before I managed to get to my feet. Just *gone*. I went to check on the men that they'd been fiddling with, and by Christ, I had never seen anything like it. I've seen plenty men shot, stabbed, I even saw a fella take an arrow clean through his eyeball once. This, out in th' desert… This was different.

"All the men was dead, everyone but me, but that ain't the part that spooked me. The West is a place of death— anyone who's been here longer than a week knows *that*. Killin' and dyin' are natural, see? What *ain't* natural is whatever them tall things had been doin'. Every one of the volunteers— *every* one— had his eyes and mouth sewn shut. Stitched shut with red twine, right? And that's not the worst part. The worst part is what I saw on the bodies they hadn't finished with yet, the ones that they'd been hunkered down over."

"They had their manhoods stolen," says Left Hand, "and calves' heads sewn where their organs had been cut away, if your guests had time to get to that bit of their business before you scared them away."

Joe Peck's eyes are huge and wet and shine in the distant light of Cygnus' lamp. "Christ *alive*, it was the worst thing I'd ever seen. I ran, and kept running. After what I saw— what th' boggarts had done— killin' men seemed like even less to me than it had before that night, out in Yavapai country. But here I am. Chasing a dollar has me mixed up with devilry again. At the very least, with witchcraft."

Left Hand has listened to Joe Peck's story carefully— the volunteers on their way to kill Yavapai, the contempt and fear with which he pronounces the word "witchcraft"—and she mulls it over as they pace the perimeter.

"Well," says Joe Peck, "you hunt monsters, don't you? Have you run up against them tall ones before? Killed any of 'em?"

"I have met their kind before. I have killed their kind before—maybe a dozen, all told. I prefer not to hunt them.

241

I hunt alone, and they are never fewer than four or five in number, and never far from one another."

"I sure wish you'd been there that night," says Joe Peck. "Hunting them, I mean."

"You say you were at war with the Yavapai. But you came to their land, took it as conquerors and invaders, and murdered anyone who tried to stop you. You wish I had been there, little wašíču? I would have waited for the *Chirurgiens des Ténèbres* to have finished with your band— all of you. Then, and only then, would I have seen to their destruction. There may not have been a price set for the *Chirurgiens*. Angels rarely fetch a bounty, whatever species they be. But I bet..." Left Hand draws her good black-glass knife. It's an implement of gorgeous brutality, ten inches long, razor-sharp, and bearing a serrated edge like the teeth of a saw from Hell. It looks right at home in the light of the magician's lamp. The blade gleams wet black and liquid pink along its edge in time with the shadows.

"You and the other wašíču... I bet if I'd taken your heads as proof, the Yavapai would have paid me for *you*. It's no easy thing, crossing the desert with that many heads. I could have taken your man-parts as proof instead. Much easier to transport. But the *Chirurgiens* had already seen to those. They did not get very far in their efforts before you scared them off, by the sound of it. That's almost a shame. They consider themselves artists, you know, not monsters. Monsters sometimes know what they are— sometimes delight in it. But more often, they are just animals, just like men. They eat, they defecate, they fornicate." She grins, the edge of her scarred and puckered lip pulled back in a horrible cadaverous leer. "They die."

"You're a godless thing!" Fear and shock fight for dominance of Joe Peck's twitching features, and he takes a step back from her.

I am *alive*," she responds. "Unlike a great many people I have known. Now take your whisky and your guns, and try to be of use. Go walk the other side of the graves. And be silent, if you think you can manage it."

Joe Peck does as he's told.

¤

"You said that Christiansen was here, was alive some-how. We buried him, father— I was *there*, in case you for-get. I remember the work that night in Winter Quarters well. Those were my brothers and sisters, although I didn't know it yet. It has been good to think, over the years, that I helped return Christiansen to the earth, to wait for resurrection."

"Oh, he rose from the grave, all right." Leonidas issues a harsh barking laugh— a spasm of mirth that sounds pain-ful. "Although resurrection *per se* had nothing to do with it. The shambling thing you'll see tonight never died at all— not truly."

"I don't understand it," says Miles. The hurt in his voice is genuine.

"Hmmm. *What* don't you understand, exactly?"

"The second anointing. He and his wife— Eliezer and Eufenia— were given the second anointing by proxy and raised to the highest path of the plan of salvation. How can that be, when he still lives—worse, when he crawls the earth by night, a mockery of Heavenly Father's natural man? It makes no *sense*."

"No sense whatsoever," Leonidas agrees. "And that's for the simple reason that your faith is a cracked crock of ridiculous nonsense, dreamed up by a lustful, fancy little man—"

In extremis, Leonidas has observed, the human animal rarely manages to hold onto dignity, rarely, in fact, even holds onto its differentiation from the sound of the slaughterhouse, the squeal of pigs and moaning of cows led to the knife. The sound that pierces the chill night air is one such noise— a horrible, liquid, abattoir scream of pain and terror, high-pitched, gurgling, and unmanned. Punctuating this ghastly vocal solo is a twin explosion— *POK-POK*— of gunfire. The racket cuts off Leonidas' diatribe as neatly as if it had been cleft by a knife. From behind Brimelow, Left Hand's voice is mild and indifferent.

"Your guest is here."

Chapter Thirteen

There can be no mistake regarding the sound that follows Joe Peck's liquid animal screams— at least, no mistake for those who have heard it before. *The sweet music of the ghūl. There is some of that two-headed lamb to it*, Leonidas thinks, remembering, again, the day when his father had taken him to the neighbor's farm to see the deformed animal. *But there's more of the man to it than I thought I heard in Winter Quarters. It's the sound of a man* in extremis, *but I have almost heard its match from a human throat. Perhaps that labor agitator in Marquette. He made an entire zoo's worth of sounds when the Pinkertons had finished with his fingers and begun work on his genitals with pliers and knives.* The strike leader had been a stubborn man, stubborn enough to warrant a transcontinental journey by Leonidas the Great Man. It wasn't often that he took such a personal interest in a dispute that he'd stir himself to supervise such treatment personally. The agitator had been a tough nut, all right, but in the end, he had bent and broken, as all men do when the proper pressure is applied. *This will be just like that, easier, even*, he assures himself. The call of the *ghūl* fills the chilly air with its terrible resonance, the sound of a half-swallowed tongue vibrating in a thick throat, distorted through misshapen sinuses. It comes once— then a second time, nearer their little quadrant of graves. Then, moving slowly and low to the ground, Christiansen's pale form swims out of the darkness.

Had Leonidas thought the thing in Winter Quarters loathsome? Had he doubted Cygnus' description of the thing which had launched itself out of the tomb, shrieking, in Giza? If so, the sight of Christiansen— of what was once, previously Christiansen— disabuses him of this notion. He had not known horror, nor imagined it. The thing found its

247

way to them, after all. After twenty years of squalor spent writhing in an excremental, reeking burrow, twenty years at the banquet table of rotting human flesh eaten in the dark, of foulness so potent that even death will not embrace it— after all this, and after twenty years of blood and gold, their paths have crossed again.

Christiansen's limbs are warped out of true in jagged zigs and zags. Hopelessly twisted, he scuttles and shuffles sideways, low to the ground like an albino crab. His skin is as white as an albino salamander's beneath a smeared rime of dirt (*grave dirt*, thinks Leonidas), and his bulbous skull is pulled out of true. His jaw is only able to close partway, being severely bent to one side; a constant runner of thick foam bubbles from it and down what would, on a skull not so grievously deformed, perhaps be called a chin. Everywhere on his frame, the bone-white skin is stretched taut over the unhappy congress of his bones. He is emaciated beyond the point at which a fully mortal man would have died, his skin little more than a leathery sheath clinging to his skeleton. His eyes are two opaque marbles in his head, but something burns deep within them— a colorless spark with an uneasy effervescence. His eyes *do* express shards of something that had been entirely absent in Abner and the thing in Winter Quarters: human consciousness, of a sort. Christiansen scuttles nearer the square of graves with their shovels, the circle of light cast by Cygnus' lantern, and as he does so, he comes bearing a gift.

Thus ends the ballad of Joe Peck, gun for hire, thinks Leonidas. Joe's throat and jaw are mostly gone. So much of the flesh has been ripped away that the greasy white knobs of his spine peek through the morass of meat below his upper lip. There are large holes ripped in the upper arms of his jacket, with chunks of both suit and flesh bitten away. Joe Peck's wounds still weep blood, although he is quite dead. His eyes bug from his head, capillaries burst by the force and horror of his end. *I'd wager that's a grievous enough wound to help poor Joe stay dead,* Leonidas thinks. He has, much to his surprise, begun to sweat in the extremity of a quite unexpected emotion: fear. *Even so, we shall have to burn his body. To be certain.*

"How does he not see us? Or hear us?" Leonidas is star-

249

tled to hear how calm Lehi sounds. He had been sure that, upon seeing the partially-eaten Joe Peck, the boy would lose his guts. Instead, it's his father that has been reduced to a trembling jelly. Lehi sounds fascinated. *He has grown up in the West. Out here, in the empty places, among these little archipelagos in an ocean of death*, Leonidas thinks. *He is no soft New York boy*.

"My little lantern is certainly nothing when compared to Aaron's lamps. Isn't that right, boy?" Despite the bored drawl that Cygnus affects, Leonidas can see the sweat bead on his forehead and knows that the magus, too, is disconcerted by the sight of Christiansen. "Still, the light provided by my friend here obscures us from our monster. For now. Settle in, young master Pyburn. You're not without Talent. I can smell it on you. Let's see what you make of a *real* working— let's see what you make of my light-storm."

¤

Left Hand still does not understand what the ghosts want from her, if indeed they could be said to *want* anything in their condition. She had long ago erroneously supposed that the act of wanting, of wanting *anything*, was beyond them.

Surely it had to be so, what with the specters being little more than echoes of echoes, stubborn stains on the material of the living world. She knows better now. Many ghosts have lost everything *but* hunger. Appetite is the last thing that leaves them, especially those that died badly, and the preceding decades have overflowed with bad deaths, ugly deaths. Deaths that leave behind hungry ghosts, the cold and ravenous dead. In her travels for the hunt, she has often seen their pale forms lingering in the shadows. She has even tried to converse, to find reason in the black pits of their eyes on a few occasions. The dead do not socialize, nor do they find comfort in each others' presence; as a rule, they keep to the darkness in bitter isolation. The most of them she has ever seen in one place was on the day she burned the unclean cave with Little Eagle by her side. Left Hand had survived that encounter only by sheer luck. Little Eagle had not been so fortunate. She supposes that Little Eagle's ghost may be among those that roam the maple groves, even now. *That* had been a crowd of the dead, a surprising thing out in the isolation of the woods but understandable, given the corruption that slept there. The ghosts had hated the nest of grave-robbers, perhaps because theirs was a species whose life-bread was the desecration of corpses, the defilement of spirit.

Compared to the crushing wave that fills the cemetery now, that throng of ghosts had been no more than a handful. This, in the City Cemetery, is more of them than she has ever seen. They throng the thing that now slouches into view, the thing the wašíču insist on giving the Cannibal God's name—Christian's Son. They throng him in an unruly tide, although he doesn't seem aware of them. To her, they do not look like they belong in the cemetery; they do not feel part of the place. They feel bereft, lost, misplaced. Brimelow had been quite stingy with details about Christian's Son— he had only conveyed that the creature had quite a distance to travel to get to Great Salt Lake City. Perhaps it has been picking them up on its way, one adhering to it here, one there, like tumbleweeds clogging a narrow gully in the wind. *That* doesn't feel quite right to her either, though. They feel of a piece—but a piece ripped from its home and transplanted here. The ghosts collide and bounce off of the tombstones, careen against each other, reach and grasp at Christian's Son and the markers alike with long, sticky limbs and fingers. Try as they might, they cannot seem to grasp or push against the material world. Most of them settle for swirling around Christian's Son like a syrup vortex, or a swirling stew of boiled, half-disassembled fruit.

"The dead are no help to the living"— had she actually said that, once? The truth is that the dead are often of *great* help to the living, much more than the living ever were to them. She has found that some of the dead are malign, or simply incomprehensible in their pleasures and political beliefs. Many are driven by hunger or other physical needs, the way this Christian's Son is. It— unlike the others of its kind that she has dispatched over the years— still retains a rotten phosphorescence in its eyes, the vestigial residue of thought. *Is this*, she wonders, *why the ghosts follow him? Why they reach for him with desperate, clinging arms, with hands that can never touch him?*

"Can *they* see us?" Pyburn's grandson asks the corrupted wizard.

"Can *who* see us? Never mind that—pipe down for now, young man. We've reached the moment of truth."

The boy sees the ghosts, Left Hand marvels. The sorcerer's sight can be penetrating, she has heard, but only when he travels as the thing that lives inside him. With her own in-born Talent, she perceives the wizard's parasite— a being like a melting pane of glass engulfed by flame. With his attention fixed on Christian's Son and the burning window inside of him shut tight, the wizard does not see— *cannot* see—the dead that follow in their visitor's wake.

Christian's Son drops Joe Peck to the cemetery earth with a slumping thud. The would-be Indian killer's eyes are full of blood, horror stamped upon what's left of his face. The creature pauses, still a short distance from the circle of the lantern's pulsing light and the chairs occupied by the Pyburn men. It raises its misshapen head to the night air, so redolent of freshly turned earth and the green life of spring (now laced with an undertone of gunpowder and blood), and flares its lopsided nostrils. It catches a scent and cranes its head in the direction of the Pyburns. A low, rumbling growl

254

begins in its throat; it sounds like stones falling one over another at the beginning of a landslide. It draws nearer, step by step, until, finally, it steps into the inner circle of the lantern's rays. Once the pink light washes over it, Christian's Son's clouded, stony eyes, with their dancing points of light, their dim cognizance, fix upon the Pyburns. Its face crunches up horribly, and it takes Left Hand but a moment to realize that the hideous expression it bears is what passes for joy in the creature's life: *there* they are, its long-lost friends, at last!

The thing drops to all fours and breaks into a shambling, lopsided run, directly at Leonidas, Lehi, and Miles.

¤

"Hold fast!" Leonidas barks. *Is that intended to shore* them *up or to stiffen my own spine*? "Frater Cygnus, it's time to prove yourself worthy!"

Sweaty though he be, Cygnus stands his ground just ahead of the Pyburns. Behind Leonidas, Brimelow mutters the Lord's Prayer; this is something that Leonidas notes in an abstract way for later consideration. *I would have thought the Catholicism driven out of him by the things he has seen in my*

255

employ, he thinks. *Maybe he has been turned back to popery by the things that he has* done *in my employ.* "Merciful Father, protect me," cries Miles as Christiansen breaks into a run, and Leonidas enjoys a moment of bitter amusement in which he is unsure whether the entreaty is directed at him or at the Almighty. *I suppose neither of us is particularly merciful,* he thinks. Christiansen's charge brings him within the area bounded by the four graves, each with its burlap-wrapped shovel. The trap is sprung.

Cygnus' hand darts to the earth, quick as a snake, and rises holding a bundle of thick wires. He pulls as hard as he can, stripping the burlap sacking from the shovel-handles. Beneath are four lanterns, each wrought from gleaming silver filigreed with inscrutable runes, each blazing with a cold luminescence, each a different color: bright, eye-searing violet, a red deeper and murkier than blood, the green of a poisoned wormwood star, and the pure, bone-bleaching yellow of a desert sun. A spark swims in the glassy black head of the sorcerer's walking stick, then crackles with a lively fire that casts its own light in the maelstrom of color now enclosing the Pyburns, Christiansen, Brimelow, and Cygnus. He speaks a single phrase in a language that Leonidas does not understand or recognize, and unleashes what he had, to Lehi, called his "light-storm."

The eye-searing colors produced by the lamps take on a substance, a physical weight akin to a fog or vapor, and begin to swirl in a circle around the group, slowly at first. As they do, Cygnus sets his pink lantern upon the ground and reaches into its open top. Had a flame burned inside, he would have scorched his fingers. Instead, he withdraws from the glass enclosure an object whose weird radiance continues to pulse in a steady rhythm. As the light recedes within the magus' grip, Leonidas can discern that he is holding what looks like a human heart. A rather *small* human heart. *Did that*, Leonidas wonders, *come from a* child? Whatever its provenance, the heart continues, improbably, to beat, divorced as it is from vessels or a home within a body. Instead of blood, it pumps a light that contributes to the swirl surrounding the group.

The light has an immediate and physical effect upon

Christiansen. He shudders, and his pace slows as though its legs are mired in quicksand. The circle of light whirls and pulses, composed of discrete illuminations in each lantern's color, which form bands like Saturn's rings. Leonidas marvels at the sight. *Will I ever*, he thinks, *stop underestimating my pet wizard?* Heart in one hand, staff in the other, Cygnus raises his arms. At this prompt, the fog of light condenses and coalesces with an audible sizzle, then bursts into a diffuse cloud of uniform white light. This new, softer illumination has an even more pronounced effect on Christiansen. The ruined sexton begins to mewl in fear, frozen. Cygnus lifts his arms even higher. Christiansen, transfixed and entirely frozen now, floats gently into the air and hangs with his dangling feet a foot above the soil of the cemetery. His fingers twitch spastically; the flailing of the remaining claws on his truncated hand is like the death agony of a crippled spider. The air is filled with the tactile sensation of a diffuse lightning storm and the distinctive smell of burning sugar.

"*There* we are, Mr. Pyburn, just as I assured you. The first step was the hardest. But he's set foot in our trap, and we've sprung it. Mr. Brimelow, the grimoire?"

Brimelow, prayers forgotten, is already elbow-deep in the satchel. He withdraws a somewhat tattered-looking leather-bound book and flips to a bookmarked page before holding it up before the magus where he can read aloud. Cygnus begins muttering. The words sound like the same inscrutable language as before to Leonidas, but, as he is well aware, he is no scholar of languages. Leonidas has found the accented English of his Welsh miners and Chinese laborers difficult enough to understand, on the few occasions he has had the misfortune to be subjected to their company.

Cygnus' murmured incantation continues. His voice, ordinarily a mellow contralto, has taken on a strange depth of tone, as though his vocal chords are being pulled out of true by the words passing through them. Leonidas can see on the magician's face that the process of pronouncing his spell is a physically painful one; sweat rolls off of him in rivulets, and his blonde ringlets have begun to adhere to his forehead. The effect is not unlike a ring of laurels adorning the head of a bust of Caesar.

"Oh, they are Saints," Lehi cries with rapturous horror. It is unclear to Leonidas whom the boy is addressing or what on Earth he's babbling about. "Are these their Telestial bodies? And what are they *doing* here? No, no, this is all *wrong*."

"Be quiet, boy," growls Brimelow, cutting a glance at the youth. All he can do is growl. After all, for the moment, he must remain glued to his place before Cygnus, holding the book.

"But what do they *want*? And what are they *doing*? They are not young, not restored to health. Heavenly Father, where are their *mouths*? Why are their arms so long, why do their hands reach like that?" Lehi sounds heartbroken more than fearful, sick with sadness. *What in God's name is wrong with the boy?* Leonidas wonders. Although it pains him, he remembers Abner when he had been a child, the conversations with imaginary friends and angels that Leonidas had written off to youthful fancy.

"Your grandfather and his stained spirit-breaker cannot see them." Left Hand's words are quiet, emphatic, and without a doubt, meant for Lehi's ears. She is ignored by the other men at the heart of the low-burning white radiance. They stare, transfixed with wonder, at the miraculous events unfolding before their eyes. "I do not know what they want. They probably do not want *you*, if that is any comfort."

"We were to be family, sealed for time and all eternity, a community caring for one another through the plan of salvation. Not this. Not whatever *this* is."

"For the last time, shut it, you," warns Brimelow.

"They are just strays," Left Hand says, but her voice betrays her uncertainty, and the statement emerges in a tone that is almost a question.

"They are the sanctified dead," says Lehi, and Left Hand recognizes the dreamy tone in his voice. *The boy is a born hunter*, she thinks. *He has eyes for it even sharper than mine, and by the sound of him now, he can go deeper than me, deeper even than the soiled wizard, and all without even being aware of what he is about.* "Clad in their raiment— can't you see? They are dressed for the Resurrection, but oh, oh, their eyes are *empty*, and their mouths are *gone*." The attention from the boy seems to have stirred the ghosts into an even further state of agitation; they churn in a circle around the limp, dangling form of Christian's Son, suspended above the grave-dirt.

"This is the moment," says the sorcerer, "that you have been waiting for, Leonidas. Why don't you stand and approach our friend here? Carefully, now." Leonidas rises with a grimace and makes his stiff, careful way forward until he stands a few paces in front of Christian's Son. "Most excellent," says Cygnus, his face split by a wide, crinkled grin. The light in whose floating midst they are conducting the ritual is not flattering. In its shifting, directionless glow, every wrinkle and line that surround his eyes and the thin spread of his lips are visible. He looks, Left Hand thinks, older in that moment than any man she has ever seen. Mirthless good cheer shines in his eyes.

"This," cries the wizard in a ringing voice, bringing his staff down in a sharp arc against the ground, "do I conclude my Great Work!"

Next, the explosion, followed in short order by agonized screams.

Chapter Fourteen

Leonidas comes back to his senses like a man struggling to find his way home in a fog bank, unsure of what the shapes before him in the half-darkness are or where his path lies. He is as dazed as though he has taken a hard blow to the head, though he is no pain. The light-storm, dispersed in the explosive blast, has given way to the dim, shifting light cast by the sundered remnants of the lanterns. The pretty stained glass that had provided the colored tinge to their light is shattered, blown out across the black earth of the graves. The fragments are scattered before each lantern like a gleaming handful of jewels. The lamp's filigreed silver frames are bent and tarnished and gutter with dying orange flames. The shovel-handles, now chewed-looking, lean drunkenly.

Standing in the midst of the graves, Leonidas blinks. He stares down at his hands. They still bear the wrinkled stamp of age. He feels, he decides, no different, certainly no younger. On the other hand, while his joints are still stiff and painful, his bones have not been warped and pulled out of true. His humanity, if such could be ascribed to him to begin with, appears intact. The transfer had been intended to strip the *ghūl* of its longevity and strength, leaving only the unclean shell, which the magus had assured Leonidas would be as easily disposed of as the shed skin of a snake. What has gone wrong?

Speak of the devil— or, at least, of Cygnus. As Leonidas' senses return to him, he becomes aware that the sorcerer, unlike him, has been dealt a truly bad turn by the failed ritual. He lies where he has been transfixed, struck to the ground. There he writhes, his shrill screams of agony cleaving the night. He clutches his smoking face with half-melted hands from which vapor and the savory smell of fried pork rise in clouds, well-spiced with a stench that is reminiscent of brimstone. It would appear that whatever force had been flowing through the lanterns and into the trap had found its lightning-rod in the form of the unfortunate wizard. Leonidas cannot feel contempt for the man, however. The night's project was obviously a failure, but, just as obviously, Cygnus had proven himself capable of generating—if not controlling— tremendous power. If he could do it once, he could do it again. The battle was lost in spectacular fashion, but the war would not be over until Leonidas succumbed to the reaper's embrace. What had Cygnus called the attempt to wrest everlasting life from the stained clutches of the ghūl, his "Great Work?" Well, until the magus or Leonidas expired, the Work would continue, whether Cygnus wanted it to or not. *It may even have to continue once one or both of us are dead*, Leonidas thinks and has a single cold instant of self-doubt. *What am I* saying? *What does that even* mean? It only lasts a moment. *Tonight*, he decides, *was a mishap. Mishaps, major or minor, are a part of any undertaking.*

Leonidas remembers one incident, a few years before

his mines had begun to employ Alfred Nobel's dynamite in place of blasting powder. The men had sunk a deep shaft into the rock that stood between them and a vein of precious ore. They had packed the bottom of the shaft with powder, laid wire, and sealed the rest of the shaft with good, soft clay, rammed as tight as it could be compressed. When they'd withdrawn the wire and set the blast-man to work, things had gone awry, somehow. The charge had detonated before the mine had been cleared of workers. These mishaps were hardly unheard-of and were widely considered a cost of pulling wealth out of the miserly rock—but a run of good luck had convinced Leonidas that his enterprises were immune to the whims of the gods of dynamite. The premature detonation had instantly incinerated the ignoble explosives man, leaving not so much as a mist upon the blackened walls of rock. The accident had killed two miners in addition to the dynamite man and permanently maimed one more besides. In the end, who was left to take the blame, with the miner responsible gone up in the flash? Leonidas supposes that many of the men blamed *him*, but the depth of his scorn for this idea— that *he* was somehow responsible— is difficult to convey. There had been the mutterings of Labor agitation after that, and, following like carrion crows after a battle, Leonidas' Pinkertons had become involved.

Leonidas is glad that it seems his wizard survived the cataclysm. He is also cruelly glad that it appears the explosion has horribly injured him. So much time, poured into this effort. So much money, so much of everything, but most of all…. So much of his precious attention.

"*Lady Nyx, have mercy upon Your humble servant!*" Cygnus twists in the dirt. His white-blond curls, wet with sweat, are soon grimed with dirt. "I entreat You, primal goddess! I, who have slain for and am sealed to your most secret mysteries!" This last cry descends into either broken gibberish or a language Leonidas does not recognize. *Is he* praying? Leonidas marvels. *I suppose that* in extremis *even those who fancy themselves theological mercenaries want their Mother.*

"Be quiet!" he snaps at Cygnus. The fog in Leonidas' head begins to lift, and he attempts to take stock of the aftermath of the aborted working.

The dying lamp-light offers a bit of illumination, but after the blinding brightness of Cygnus' botched act of sorcery, it now feels very dark in the Cemetery. Leonidas grits his teeth and waits for his eyes to adjust. How much time elapsed while he was dazed? It is impossible to say. Christiansen has vanished completely— not what the Pyburn patriarch expected but far from the worst outcome, provided that the *ghūl* isn't just slinking around further out in the shadows, waiting for his opportunity to strike. Left Hand has also vanished. Leonidas makes a mental note to have her slain. She had been no help whatsoever and had been mouthy and petulant, besides. Perhaps the tiny fraternity of those dedicated to tracking and hunting the unnatural needed a reminder of who Leonidas Pyburn is and what exertions he is capable of. Speaking of having people slain, there is Mr. Brimelow. He rises from the ground where he had been knocked by the explosion of light. Lehi sits exactly where he has been seated all along. Miles is… where *is* Miles?

Then Leonidas spies him. Miles is on all fours, scrabbling in the dirt, of course. For a moment, Leonidas feels disgust and shame. Did he really sire this mewling excuse for a man? And what paroxysms of hysterical whining would this son of his enter into *now*? Then Leonidas spies the corpse of Joe Peck and realizes— too late— what Miles is about. Miles rises to his knees with Joe Peck's revolver— the one that the dead gunfighter *hadn't* dropped, in his death throes, the one that had remained clutched in his dying hand. Miles points it directly at Leonidas, who can see down the bore all the way to the cylinder. The barrel is fixed on Leonidas' face like the black and vacant eye of God.

"You are going to *listen* to me now, you are going to *listen* while I speak!" The veins stand out on Miles' broad forehead; his eyes, blue as a desert sky, are wide, his shoulders tensed. "God has *damned* you, father! Whatever it is you tried to accomplish here, do you *see* how it ended? As all hubris ends, when man challenges the divine, as at Babel, as when the Nephites were broken and scattered!" Miles draws back the hammer on Joe Peck's revolver, and Leonidas feels his bowels pucker with real fear. *Is he going to kill me, here in this godforsaken nowhere-place, this cemetery in a cemetery in a cem-*

269

etery?

"Just a moment, Miles. Do not do anything you will regret—and you *will* regret rash action here, trust me. Instead, why don't we parlay about the real meat on the bone? We can talk about *inheritance.* Since it appears that I have been stymied in my quest to avoid the grave, we Pyburns must live on, our name should survive! Your boy could be the patriarch of a great, rich clan of Latter-Day Saints! This young city— this young faith— you have a chance to truly set your hands upon the clay while it is still unformed. Do not throw that away!"

The bitterness in Miles' answering laugh could curdle milk. "Oh, I think I have the measure of you better than *that.* You will not cease trying to escape the grave until you are ensconced in it—and even then, I half-expect you take measures to see that your foul experiments continue beyond your lifespan." Tears steal from the corner of his eyes. "I shall pray for you, father, and for myself. Perhaps in the eternal progression of our souls beyond this world, we shall meet again, though I should not count on it. Take solace in this much: our name shall survive quite well in industrious poverty. And our family will certainly survive quite well without *you* — "

Miles is not quite all of the way through his last sentence when Brimelow jams the big knife sideways through the meat of his throat. Brimelow then gives the knife a savage yank, freeing it from Miles' neck and releasing an arterial cascade. There is hardly time for Miles' face to register surprise before it slackens. The gun, forgotten, falls from his hand as he drops to the ground. The eternal progression— indeed, the very existence— of the human soul is a weighty topic and one on which the opinions of learned and well-meaning gentleman may differ. What is not subject to debate is that Miles Pyburn's mortal life ends there at Brimelow's feet in a matter of moments. A small rill of blood seeps from one corner of his mouth, and though his eyes stare, wide, into the star-infested void overhead, the general cast of his face is one of a man at peace with his fate.

Leonidas watches his son bleed out. *It should have been him back at Winter Quarters. If he'd had the stones to stand and do combat with that foul thing, his brother wouldn't have given*

271

his life to save him. To save him, and for what? Dead, here, twenty years later. And what's the difference? He feels cold, and sick, and lonely, but these feelings are hollow, glassy things, easily crushed to jagged shards and swallowed. Brimelow stares at Leonidas with the watchful, slightly spooked expression of one who knows he has placed an enormous wager and is waiting to see if it pays off or bankrupts him. *I suppose I could let him stew a little while longer*, Leonidas thinks, but he grants Brimelow a tiny, stiff-necked nod, as though to say, "It was an ugly job, but it had to be done." In their distraction, neither Brimelow nor Leonidas notice as Lehi rises from his chair, then kneels beside his father, silent. Once he is already at the still-cooling corpse, Brimelow spots him. "Now, boy," he begins, backpedaling a few steps.

Lehi looks up, his eyes clear, his mouth set, and raises the gun…

…Raises it, butt-first, and hands it to a disbelieving Brimelow. Leonidas watches this with great interest.

"Ah, boy, I wish it hadn't had to be that way," Brimelow says to Lehi and pockets the gun.

"Leave the bodies, and let us make our way out of this fair city as quickly as possible," Leonidas says to Brimelow.

"*Leave* them? Two murdered men, right out in the open? And the two bodies we left at the hotel? This is rough country, Mr. Pyburn, but there's more law here than there is in Dakota or some desert hell-hole. The city fathers are would-be high priests. How do you think they'll react to such butchery within a stone's throw of their Temple?"

"I intend for a powerful monsoon of gold to find its way into the pockets of the city fathers. If past experience is any indication, a relatively modest sum would be sufficient to wash away the blood left here tonight, but there's no point taking any unnecessary chances. I shall shower enough gold upon them— their businesses, their election campaigns— that by the time I'm done, they'll be able to dip their Temple in gold, should they so wish."

Cygnus' shrill screams have begun to attract attention to the Cemetery. Already, the night is dotted with torches and rings with the faint cries of men on their way. "Quiet the wizard," Leonidas tells Brimelow, then corrects himself:

273

"*Temporarily* quiet the wizard. I will need him alive, wounded though he be." Brimelow crouches over the wizard, delivers a quick uppercut that knocks him insensate with remarkable precision, and slings his unconscious body over one shoulder. "Come, Lehi," says Leonidas, "if you wish to avoid answering for your own part in all this. Can you imagine telling your poor *mother* what transpired here tonight? Or your poor *sisters*?" Lehi stares at the ground, misery etched on his face, and looks for a moment like the not-child, not-yet-man that he is. In that instant, even Brimelow's expression softens a bit, but Leonidas spares not so much as a soft word. Instead, he regards the scion of his diminished clan with his bright blue eyes, eyes which contain as much pity as those of a hyena or a centipede. "You have seen things tonight that cannot be unseen— you *know* things, now, that cannot be *unknown*. It's time to put this place behind you. There is much the world can offer other than 'fellowship.'" He pauses, scrutinizing Lehi's young face. "For example— I can offer you *knowledge*. Secrets that even your god doesn't know." Leonidas extends one hand to the boy.

Lehi shudders, once, and then takes the old man's hand and, for the first time, assumes his place at his grandfather's side.

¤

"Natten… Natten och festen…"

He is as naked as the day he was born and almost as disoriented. The night air bites pleasurably at his skin as he stumbles among the graves, arms crossed over his chest. Arms that, for some reason, he feels should be… different. Broken or warped, somehow. Instead, his flesh is smooth and taut, his limbs are straight and strong. He has no idea where he is. Or *who* he is. But he feels, if confused, also exquisite— intoxicated, even, by the taste of the night and the strong pulse of hot blood—*his* hot blood— flowing in his veins.

"Var det en dröm?" He is aware on some level that the words are not just inside him, that he is saying them aloud. Does he know what they mean? As slow as winter ice breaking into stone, as insistent as rot eating its way through wooden beams, his memories begin to come. They jostle each

275

other in his mind, dark and toothy things. "*Nej. Ingen dröm.*" One foot before the next, he wanders drunkenly away from the commotion behind him, the screams. As he gains a little distance on that disturbance, though, he hears voices in front of him, men shouting in anxious excitement— and headed his direction. He hooks left without thinking and begins to run, crouched low enough that he hopes the scattered gravestones might provide some cover and hide his nakedness, his shame. That triggers another thought within him, flashing like fierce lightning. "*Och ingen gud på natten bortom döden. Endast oändliga månar och levande mardrömmar.*"

The low whistle of a skilled bird caller comes from the edge of the woods before him on his right. Someone is there among the trees, waving at him, beckoning with urgency. There is no time for doubt or hesitation: the voices draw ever nearer. He ducks into the woods and the waiting arms of his benefactor. She is a scar-faced Indian woman kitted out in faded leather clothes. She matter-of-factly wraps him in a buckskin coat and slips a pair of worn moccasins onto his feet. "I am Left Hand," she says. She speaks quickly, and in a low voice, but he has no trouble understanding the English she speaks. "I do not know how much you can remember. But your name is— was— Christian's Son."

Christian's Son, he thinks, and it isn't quite right. "Christiansen," he says aloud, and the clarity and sweetness of his voice astonishes him.

"Yes," she agrees and takes his hand. The buckskin coat and moccasins help abate the chill as she leads him like a child to her horse, which is hobbled not far away. Behind them, pandemonium has erupted in the Cemetery. The party of men must have found whatever wreckage Leonidas and the soiled magician left in their wake. Left Hand and Christiansen talk, voices just above a whisper, as they make their way through the trees.

"I have hunted for a long time, and I have seen many things. Wonderful things and terrible things. But I have never seen a man pulled back from living death. I do not know *what* I've seen tonight, but I suspect you are now a holy man."

"Holy man?" He thinks on this. Left Hand notes that, while the rest of his body is restored— youthful, strong, and smooth— his eyes are still two dead marbles with a terrible, burning light in their depths. *Those will need to be covered up,* she thinks, *if he wants to walk among his own kind again. If we are his own kind.* "Holy man," Christiansen says again and looks wonderingly at his hands, his smooth forearms and young, strong legs poking out from beneath the coat. He laughs, a light, joyous sound with not a hint of malice in it. "Oh, but *that* is very funny! A *holy* man. No, thank you. I have been beyond the boundaries of life and walked the night's ebony shore. I am liberated, truly free, and I serve no god."

"Well," Left Hand says, "what could be more holy than that?"

Chapter Fifteen

Salt Lake City, 1892

"Here comes the Twentieth Century, I suppose." Leonidas' voice is coarse-seasoned by age. It climbs a little higher with every passing year. Now that he is in his eighth decade, it has become almost as high as it was when he was a young man. His voice has none of that youthful sweetness, however; it is as sour as a bowl of turpentine. He regards the clang and gleam of the trolleys untrustworthy. He even regards the barbershop that occupies the glass-fronted corner of the White House Hotel with suspicion. It shines as brightly with its electric lights as an artificial box full of noonday radiance.

He stands in front of it, the same structure that had been the Delmonico Hotel on his last visit. On that visit, just as on this one, he'd been accompanied by Mr. Brimelow, although Brimelow doesn't carry the baggage this time. That duty falls to Lehi, who trails the two of them by a few paces. Brimelow's hair has turned a steely grey, and he is a thinner man than he used to be, hollowed out by the decades and by a stomach that worsens a little with each year. He still accompanies Leonidas everywhere he goes, as loyal, persistent, and reliable as a shadow. A decade earlier, Leonidas fled San Francisco south to Cambria, to a remote and ornate mansion so unusual and so mysterious that the locals had dubbed it "Pyburn Castle." And there, in his castle, Mr. Pyburn had wished to stay, safe behind walls and gates and his pet police force. Not here, in Salt Lake City (no longer "Great," he was informed), staring up at the White House Hotel with genuine contempt.

"Say, Lehi." Brimelow claps the younger man on the shoulder and smiles. "Doesn't your old Ma live around here?"

280

"We've no time," snaps Leonidas. "We're here on business, Mr. Brimelow, not so that my grandson can stage a family reunion."

"She lives in Provo," Lehi says to Brimelow. "South of here, with her new husband and his children. They've fifteen mouths to feed. I'm the last thing my mother needs. She buried her memories of me with my father."

"Your father— my son Miles—has been dead for a long time. Hmmm. Regrettable." Leonidas coughs.

"I still don't understand how you got dragged here," Brimelow says. "You're not one to chase after wild geese, Mr. Pyburn. That's what you have the Pinkertons for."

"The Pinkertons are expensive. That's why I keep you around, Brimelow. You work cheap."

That stings. Brimelow sighs and turns to Lehi. "I'll talk to the desk man and get the bags up to the suite." And, with that, Brimelow is gone.

"He's right," says Lehi. He has grown into a handsome man with hair as black as a crow's wing, a broad forehead, and bright, inquisitive blue eyes. Beyond that, any resemblance to his late father ends. He is slender and clad in clothes that are, without being flashy, worth a small fortune. Miles Pyburn may have been born in the East, but he had lived a goodly portion of his life in rough places. He had been a pioneer in a largely hostile landscape. Lehi, by contrast, now bears the stamp of decades of upper-class life, despite the rugged circumstances of his birth. His hair is neatly cut and coiffed, he is clean-shaven, and his boots are spotless. A closer look at his face might reveal a bit more about the years he has spent away from Utah Territory, in the exacting tutelage of the scarred and blinded Cygnus. His bright eyes are watchful and have the slightly dead quality of one who has seen too much. Lehi's fingers are busy with rings inscribed with symbols of power, and his bolo tie is threaded through a gleaming silver replica of a crow's skull.

"What, exactly, is Mr. Brimelow right about?" Leonidas asks once they are ensconced in the hotel's bar. "Brimelow's right that it's not like you to jump when someone snaps their fingers. Yet here we are. I don't think I've ever seen you as froggy as you were the day you got that letter."

"Ha-ha."

"Ha-ha," Lehi echoes. "Ha-ha how about you tell me? Now that we are evidently hours from this appointment."

"I have taught you much, or tried to, at least. Do you remember your first lesson in blackmail?"

Lehi smiles. "You said that it's never wise to use just the carrot or the stick. That if you have dirt on a fellow, things go smoother if you can also offer him something he wants. Provided that he bends the knee."

"Provided that he bends the knee. Hmm. Yes. Well, in my case, it's not important that you know the carrot or the stick, just that I've been, in a word, cornered. Someone knows much, much more about me than they ought— secrets that could put my comfort in more serious jeopardy than that posed by a little trip to this, the land of the Celestial Wedding. Although, I've been informed by my men here that there are whispers that the Harem of the Saints will not last much longer— that perhaps the Almighty shall intervene and ease the way for his children to enter the United States, if not into His Kingdom."

"So the carrot and the stick led you here."

"It's complicated, boy, but suffice it to say that I've been offered a trade. The security of some of my more sordid secrets and a new lead to follow regarding the Great Work. A quite promising lead."

"I suspect that you'll never admit that your quest to live forever has failed, even on your death bed," marvels Lehi. "And you are willing to trust a blackmailer?"

"That is indeed how this epistolary relationship began. But I am now engaged in a trade, and trade is something I understand. My correspondent's request was simple: I am to turn over Cygnus to his custody, and in exchange, he will gift me the exact components that have been missing from our most recent experiments."

Lehi looks gobsmacked. "You're going to 'give' this man Cygnus? Jesus *God*, grandfather, Cygnus isn't a *dog*!"

"Indeed—a dog I could have put down by now. Cygnus is blind, half-crippled, and these days he has a list of chemical requirements as long as my leg. His morphine consumption alone has become an exorbitant expense, insignificant to me, but still a nuisance to absorb. His Eye has grown crazed and developed selenoplexia. What would he do without a master whose rich blood he can suck?"

Lehi frowns into the glass of whisky before him. It is the only one he has ordered, and he has taken not so much as a sip. He watches the slow decomposition of the ice as it dilutes the liquor. "So it's to be the wizard for a bag of secrets, yours and theirs? Why am *I* here? And why didn't we bring Cygnus, if we're handing him over?"

"The instructions were explicit. Cygnus was to be left in that fetid little flat he haunts in San Francisco, where my new friend's men will pluck him up. And I was to bring only you and Mr. Brimelow here to Utah Territory— which was fine with me. Brimelow's killed more men than the plague, and you are fast becoming quite the sorcerer, Lehi. My hope is that we can handle any trouble that arises, but I do not foresee any on the horizon. We've traveled without using the Pyburn name, and unlike that damned fool Rockefeller, I've endeavored to keep my name and face *out* of the papers, besides. We are here incognito, boy, and we'll be gone by sunset tomorrow."

"Well," Lehi says, rising from his untouched and now melted glass of whisky. "I'm going to go check in on Brimelow. Will you be all right here on your own for a moment or two?" His answer from Leonidas is a contemptuous sneer.

¤

Brimelow, in the suite, is slumped in a chair that he dwarfs with his broad frame. Though he is older, reduced in bulk, and a little more faded-looking than the last time he visited the White House (formerly the Delmonico), Brimelow is still an imposing man. Lehi, in a move that would almost certainly irritate his grandfather, immediately tells him of the blackmail and the deal to trade Cygnus for materials related to the Great Work. He is not sure what reaction he expected, but it wasn't for Brimelow to slump even lower in his seat with a pained expression on his face. The big bodyguard asks Lehi a single question.

"Do you think it is *right*, what he's doing?"

"Is that the first time you've ever asked yourself that

question, Brimelow?" Lehi responds. "At any rate, we're waiting for word from this new fellow's men in San Francisco, so the die is cast already. I gather we are to attend a preliminary meeting tonight." He pats the big man on the arm. "Why don't you take it easy up here? I have a feeling the old man is apt to be crueler than usual. I'm young and too green to know when I'm being insulted." He tips Brimelow a wink.

Brimelow laughs. "Aye. I'll tell you what—I'm going to do that. Do not leave the hotel without collecting me."

"Don't worry. Can you imagine him seeing this thing through without you by his side?"

¤

When Lehi rejoins him at the bar, Leonidas' face is grim, and it quickly becomes apparent that he has been drinking steadily. The sole head—the tyrant— of the Pyburn Empire looks regal. His travel clothes can't hide the bearing that a half-century of wealth, power, and the acid inadequacy of the nouveau riche have driven into him. He also looks dyspeptic. *Did he eat the wrong thing on the train ride?* But no— the expression he sees on Leonidas' face, Lehi realizes, is nervousness.

Lehi has hardly taken his seat when an unobtrusive member of the wait-staff slides over, silent and graceful as an owl in the night. "Mister… Lazarus?" he asks. Lehi had thought it a ridiculous name to travel under. The valet deposits a small crème-colored envelope before Leonidas, who seizes it and tears it open at once. He reads the slip of paper inside, and it's as though he ages ten more years in half a minute, right before Lehi's eyes. "*Bastards,*" he growls. He grimaces like a man seized by terrible indigestion and grips the bar with his broad hands. Their flesh is dried up and withered like rawhide, but his tendons still possess enough strength that when he grips the bar and squeezes it with all his might, it creaks like a ship's timbers in the wind. The barkeep looks up from his bar-back busyness, alarmed.

"We are to meet them in the City Cemetery," Leonidas says. "At Miles' grave. And we are to hasten now, leaving Mr. Brimelow. They want both of us there, you and me. At your father's grave."

¤

Lehi looks around at the early summer day, bright but

not yet hot, warm as a lover's kiss. The trees are heavy with leaves, the air heavy with birdsong. The green stretches before them, a wide and peaceful swath dotted with markers. Most of them are modest. A few are elaborate. *The last time I was here*, Lehi muses, *was the night that father almost killed Grandfather*. As they stand before Miles' marker, he thinks *I was right not to come to his funeral. Look how modest the stone, anonymous among all of these similar markers*. Lehi cranes his neck and looks around: the only other people in sight are two grave-diggers plying their craft a few rows of graves over. A fresh plot in the earth just excavated, they've taken a well-earned rest. They lean on their shovels, caps pulled down, and mutter in quiet voices with their heads lowered. They could be praying.

As he casts his eyes around the Cemetery, Lehi takes stock of one important fact: there are no ghosts. He still sees them, sporadically (a few wander Pyburn Castle). In all his years learning at Cygnus' twisted side, he has, however, never seen anything like the wave that had followed Christiansen into the Cemetery. The lack of ghosts mooning about in the shadows indicates that those whose bodies are planted here are, as far as he knows, at peace. If not eternal progression, then at least they may have been granted oblivion. He is not sure what he believes about what follows death; he has seen much, and done much, while learning from his grandfather's pet sorcerer. He has studied and practiced his Talents until he practically surpassed the magician. Well, given Leonidas' decision, he supposes he may *have* surpassed him in his grandfather's eyes, or at least proved his equal. The lack of ghosts here tells Lehi something else, too. His father's death had been ignominious, and his burial here looked to be marked by one shoddy stone plaque in an anonymous sea. But that *belonging*, whatever it was, had given him rest among his brethren, nestled here until the last horns blew, until the Savior returned to resurrect the noble dead and reign in peace throughout the universe.

Or not. The Savior's reappearance was— in Lehi's estimation— unlikely.

"Well, here's his grave," Leonidas says, tapping on the surface of the marker with his gold-tipped cane. He glowers down at it, lost for a moment in thought. *And what* are *you thinking, grandfather*? Lehi wonders. In his lengthy tutelage in the arts of both magick and earthly power, Lehi had often wished he could read his grandfather's thoughts, but that particular Talent was not among those in his arsenal. Lehi watches his grandfather's face in silence, intent on trying to read the minute emotions there. Is there any guilt? Any remorse? Lehi can't say for sure. Whatever the feelings flitting through Leonidas, he is master of them once more after a few glum seconds of silence. He lifts his eyes from his son's grave, and whatever he had intended to say to Lehi dies in his mouth.

Lehi is staring at him, his gaze cold and even. He has withdrawn a long, razor-sharp stiletto from a sheath inside his coat. He is flanked, on his left and right, by the two "grave-diggers."

"What is this?" Leonidas asks. He intends the question to come out in a growl, but to his dismay, the sound of his voice is an old man's quavering, querulous complaint.

Lehi's smile is like the cold gleam of steel. "Oh, you

know. Nature. Vengeance. Call it whatever you wish. Cygnus devised this whole affair as one last test of your character— one which you failed."

"Cygnus," says Leonidas, "is detained."

"If you are referring to the telegram that I had sent to you, Worshipful Master Cygnus *wrote* it, you silly old goose." A grave-digger circles to each side of the lord of Pyburn Castle, cutting off any avenue of escape he may have— not that he could do much running, were the opportunity afforded him. He has become too frail.

Leonidas' mouth goes dry and works convulsively as though he is trying to chew a stone. He turns his eyes to first one grave-digger, then the other. "Whatever this murderous cur is paying you, I will…" He trails off, seeing no comprehension in the men's bloodshot eyes.

"They don't speak English," says Lehi. To the men, he says, "Mae am brynu'ch teyrngarwch," and they chuckle. "The Welsh," Lehi says to Leonidas, "have one thing in common with the Saints. They believe that some crimes—some sins—can only be answered through blood atonement." Leonidas scans the Cemetery for help, but the Welshmen and the Pyburns are the only ones in evidence.

"Kneel," says Lehi. When Leonidas balks, the men to either side of him grab his arms. They twist them and force him to his knees before the grave of Miles Pyburn.

"Do you remember what my father said to you, the night he died?"

"I… don't…"

"He was afraid of what your intentions were for me, a wise fear, as it turns out. He said that he would see you dead and buried before he saw me turned over to you. Instead, he's buried here, naught but bones after twenty years, I'd wager."

"Are you a *fool*?" Leonidas roars. His attempts to look regal and commanding are unconvincing, given the fear in his eyes and his current position, kneeling in the dirt. "I am *Leonidas Pyburn*. If you act rashly, you will regret it with much ardent suffering, and at length. Do you think a man like me just *disappears*?"

"When was the last time you left the Castle? Or spent

any time in San Francisco? No, instead, you conduct your affairs through intermediaries or by wire." Leonidas does not reply. Despite his good-humored smile, Lehi's face has all the warmth of an eel. "Why do you think your network of informants didn't alert you of the danger here? What did you think could remain hidden from Cygnus' Eye? This plan has long been in the works. At first, Cygnus and I planned for a day when you would expire naturally, would pass the baton to me, your sole heir. But the years have worn on, and you stubbornly refuse to expire— you haven't had so much as a sniffle in the long time that I've known you. Add to that natural lifespan the prospect of Leonidas Pyburn, immortal, and… well. You will never stop in the pursuit of your Great Work. Just as you said earlier this evening: the war, in your eyes, is never truly lost. So we— the wizard and myself —began to plan your usurpation.

"According to word left with the skeleton crew at Pyburn Castle, ostensibly by you, you are off seeing to a rich find in Alaska, and I am in Santa Rosa. Mr. Brimelow is back at the hotel, blissful and ignorant. When we're done here, I shall break him like a brittle twig. And then... After a suitable amount of time, I shall have you pronounced missing, and then dead, and then we shall commence our new Great Work, Cygnus and I. One unconcerned with immortality. Cygnus has looked far and deep, grandfather, and has seen things that could, if systematized, constitute an entirely new form of magicks. We are going to change the world, that grotesque little man and I."

"Lehi, my boy, my *blood*! I raised you like my *own son*!"

"I don't doubt it. In fact, I'm certain that that's why I hate you so much. Nothing that your shadow touches escapes unscarred."

A bird calls, a long, beautiful string of jubilant, articulated notes in the summer air. *The world*, thinks Leonidas, *is too beautiful to lose, to leave.*

"You can beg now, if you'd like. Cygnus said he'd like that. He's watching us right now, you know. His Eye is not afflicted with— what did you call it? Selenoplexia? No, his Eye works just fine."

Leonidas is silent.

"I suppose it's just as well. That magician *does* have a cruel streak. Tormenting you won't bring my father back— I wouldn't want to bring him back, even if I could. He's at peace. I don't know if death will bring *you* peace, grandfather, but maybe there's hope for you in a doctrine particular to this place. To the soil of this place. Perhaps if we offer atonement— if we shed your blood upon the Earth— your long, unholy string of debts may begin to be forgiven. Let's find out, shall we?"

When Lehi opens Leonidas' throat, the blood does, indeed, spill upon the soil in a pulsing flood. Enough blood to drench the dirt, in fact, more blood than he would have thought the dried-up old man had in him. When it has finished pulsing into the rich black earth of Miles' grave, the two Welshmen engage in their own bit of rapid, practiced grave-robbing. Once they've divorced his corpse of its gold tie-pin, watch, and ring, however, they stop; they've been informed beforehand of how certain events unfolded and know better than to touch the gold peacock pendant around the old man's neck. They drag Leonidas to the open, freshly-dug grave and roll him in. He is buried, bereft of a coffin, with no more ceremony than that.

Chapter Sixteen

It has been years since Lehi has required a key to open any lock he desires. "These are the true Keys to the Kingdom," Cygnus had said when he'd taught his protégé the magicks of locks and passage. In the White House Hotel, the suite door's hardy deadbolt slides open as though Lehi's touch were red hot and the metal something as malleable as paraffin or butter. The door's hinges make no sound as he pushes it gently open, revealing the room beyond. The windows are open to catch the breeze. The day is just ripening to evening, and the air is fresh. Brimelow is in an overstuffed chair at the foot of the master bed, situated where the breeze is sweetest. He dozes with his hands folded on this diminishing stomach and, in his slumber, gives voice to an occasional choked mutter. Lehi pads to the edge of the bed, sits, and regards the big man. Brimelow has been, at Leonidas' direction and at various points, his babysitter, guardian, and instructor. *And jailer*, Lehi thinks. *Don't forget jailer*.

He slides the stiletto from its place inside his coat. Although he had wiped it clean at the Cemetery, he had done so in haste, and its blade is still dark in places with his grandfather's blood. He could, he knows, stab Brimelow in the throat or the heart— the work of seconds— and tie the last remaining threads together. After a moment's thought, he returns the knife to its sheath, snaps it closed, and closes his eyes. Lehi is very still for almost a full minute. His breathing slows and deepens as he concentrates. Finally, the necessary mental architecture for the working locks into place, and power flows into his left hand. The rings he wears on those fingers grow at first warm, then hot. The tiny engraved symbols on them are almost hot enough to burn his flesh, but Lehi hardly notices.

Certain magickal equations, when coupled with the right mental architecture, open secret doors beyond which lie vast troves of unimaginable, almost limitless power. This power takes certain forms that one can seize with one's material body and put to use. The working Lehi is engaged in now is not one that a novice would attempt— at least, not if they intended to keep all of their limbs and avoid bursting into flames. But Lehi is no novice. Using a power this fierce to perform what are going to be, for him, parlor tricks would no doubt be considered reckless arrogance by some. But those who would criticize hadn't been his teachers. Those who *had* educated Lehi (beyond what he'd learned at home, before Leonidas) had only ever taught him ferocity, arrogance, cruelty, avarice, and cunning.

Except that Brimelow *had* taught him other things besides, hadn't he? Had taught him how to be funny and how to dance with girls. And Brimelow had even taught him, on a few occasions, how to show mercy. The guilt the Irishman carried with him as a reward for his loyal service to Leonidas was eating his guts out from the inside. *I am taking an enor-*

mous chance on you by letting you survive this night, Lehi thinks. *I need to make an impression. The fear of God will not suffice to keep you quiet. I am going to have to instill the fear of* me.

Lehi clenches his left fist, and the air is split by a sharp *CRACK* like timber breaking. Sparks fly from his rings, reeking, violet-colored flecks of fire that touch down on the carpet and burn holes in it. The noise wakes Brimelow, who lurches upright with a start. "Sweet *Jesus*, Lehi, what are you about?" Before he answers, Lehi flexes his fingers, and flames flow from his palm outward, engulfing his bare forearm up to the elbow. The conflagration, for all the effect it is having on Lehi, may as well be an illusion, but as Brimelow watches, a drop of liquid fire rolls off of Lehi's hand and sets a small blaze on the carpet. *That,* he thinks, *is no damned illusion.*

"I've just killed my grandfather," Lehi says, matter-of-fact as can be.

"Oh…?"

"Yes. All of this— this whole trip—was engineered to end in his murder. *And* yours."

"But now you're having second thoughts about shedding

301

my blood."

Lehi laughs and leans close to Brimelow, reaching with his flaming hand. The rings are white-hot now, but Lehi's flesh is untouched. The heat baking off of his fingers singes Brimelow's skin as he strokes his cheek, and the bodyguard— *ex*-bodyguard, now— yelps. "Oh, Brimelow. I wouldn't have to *spill* your blood. I could just boil it inside of you until you were cooked as red as a Christmas pig." The flames flowing up Lehi's hand are mesmerizing.

And, just like that, the power is released, the flames vanish. "But it needn't come to that. I think, Mr. Brimelow, that when I told you I'd killed my grandfather, your first reaction was relief. You are the master of your destiny now. Cygnus and I have great things before us— a new Great Work. You're free— as free as you want to be, at any rate. You are welcome to stay at the Castle until we've straightened out the legal niceties and I've settled up with you for your long service." Taking stock, Brimelow is surprised to find that the death of Leonidas, the man whom he served so long and so faithfully, brings no grief and no anger. He feels the eerie peace of a man who has finally managed to vomit up something that has long been making him sick.

"Lehi," he says sadly, "will you really go back to that wizard and continue what you're about with him?"

"Oh yes, Mr. Brimelow, and without my grandfather slowing us down, I expect us to make great progress."

The big man sighs. "I suppose I have an evening train west to catch. I'll aim to be cleared out by the time you get back to the Castle. I'd wish you Godspeed, but I almost believe it would be counterproductive, given the ventures you're engaged in. Goodbye, Lehi."

Moments after Brimelow leaves, taking only the clothes on his back and enough cash to get him to San Francisco, there is a soft knock at the door. Lehi answers and accepts a folded slip of paper— a telegram, sent the hour before.

LEHI: A PITY THAT LP WAS SILENT. I WOULD HAVE LIKED TO WATCH HIM BEG. – CYGNUS

¤

Lehi allows himself one day to mourn his grandfather, and he spends it roaring drunk. He has rarely touched liquor

303

in his life, but it feels like he should send the old man off with a celebration of *some* kind. He is unsure of whether he is engaged in mourning or celebration. Perhaps, he thinks, there's a little of both to be done. His hate for Leonidas and his careful planning with Cygnus notwithstanding, Lehi hadn't been sure of how he would feel with the deed done: the answer, it turns out, is that he feels numb and exhausted.

He begins the day at the White House, then— a little after noon— he wanders out of the lobby and into Salt Lake City. He thinks, vaguely, that he might head for Main Street, which he finds with no difficulty. It's strange to be in Salt Lake again. His gait is steady despite the handful of drinks he had at the White House, and he threads his way through Saints, immigrants, miners, plutocrats, newspapermen, investors, a whole class of people crowded in cacophonous co-existence— *a cacophony*, he allows, *of white people, at any rate*. This crude formulation is very clearly Leonidas speaking through him like a ghost. *A ghost no holy water will exorcize*, he thinks. *This exorcism will require whisky.*

He wanders from bar to bar; hadn't Main Street been

colloquially known as "Whisky Street" when he'd been an adolescent here? He believes so, and it still lives up to the nickname. In the late afternoon, Leonidas is forcefully ousted from a dark little tavern halfway down the block. His removal stops just short of a beating, which would arguably have been, by that point, deserved. Lehi staggers atop jellied legs and decides that a brief pause in his one-man wake for Leonidas is called for. He winds his way to a dingy little eatery and slumps into a chair near the back corner, intent on fortifying his stomach with something other than liquor before continuing the evening. Although he is obviously drunk, he is just as obviously a man of means, and thus he is treated with cautious politeness. He orders a beef steak, which materializes with such haste that it couldn't possibly have been prepared fresh. He regards the tough, leathery cut of meat with glum resignation and is just about to dig in when he feels a warm hand on his shoulder. He looks up into the radiant, beaming face of a man he does not recognize.

"Why, is that Lehi Pyburn? It has been quite some time since I laid eyes on you, young man!"

The stranger is clad in white from the crown of his head, which is adorned by a flat white straw hat, to his impeccable white leather boots. He wears a white shirt and coat and loose, blowsy white trousers, and for one instant of irrational terror, Lehi is sure that he is being visited by an angelic apparition of some kind, perhaps intent on personally dragging him to perdition to answer for his crimes. But his hand feels solid on Lehi's shoulder, and he certainly *looks* corporeal enough. And though he called Lehi "young man," the bloom of youth is in full flower on this man's face, as well. He sits without asking next to Lehi and grants him a dazzling grin laden with straight, white, evenly-spaced teeth. One feature of his outfit is *not* white, Lehi notes: the man's eyes are invisible behind round spectacles of smoked glass, tinted so dark that his gaze may as well be a pair of black holes in the jovial cosmos of his face.

Lehi does not like the fact that this man recognizes him. If Leonidas had been careful about keeping his face and name out of the papers, Lehi, by comparison, lived a life of utter and complete sequestration. Had he met this man before, perhaps across the table during a labor dispute? His speech *is* accented, although not like a Welshman's. "You've never *properly* met me before," the man says, as though reading Lehi's thoughts, "at least, not in *this* guise. We did meet, once. It was in this city, as a matter of fact. One night in the Cemetery." It is at that point that Lehi notes the missing fingers, the scarred (but youthful) hand.

He feels the room spin. "Jesus God," he breathes. "*Christiansen?*"

"I looked a bit different that night, did I not?" Christiansen asks.

"We were *sure* you had survived. My grandfather scoured the earth looking for you, trying to ascertain what had gone wrong."

"Isn't that heartening— *you* lot were trying to find *me*? As *I* was learning everything I could about *you*? Think of that! Friends who did not know they were friends, for all those years, you and me and your grandfather— and that unfortunate conjurer Cygnus." Christiansen chuckles.

"Worshipful Master Cygnus—"

307

"'Worshipful Master,' is that what he's calling himself? Oho! Hohoho!" Christiansen's laugh is boisterous but bears no sharp edges.

"… Cygnus always believed that you had survived. He assumed you were still a *ghūl*, creeping about by night somewhere, feeding on the dead. Yet he could never find you, try as he might."

"With that ravenous Eye of his, no doubt. It took me years, but with proper instruction and dutiful, studious attention, I believe I have learned everything there is to know about *you*, Lehi." Christiansen regards him from behind his black spectacles. "You and your *late* grandfather, yes?" A chill creeps up Lehi's spine. "Oh," Christiansen continues gaily, "don't worry about me, Lehi. I'm not looking for any complications. Provided that the complications in question aren't looking for *me*."

"The corruption was entirely taken from you," Lehi says wonderingly and takes Christiansen's hand. It is soft, smooth, and warm— scarred and solid. When Lehi breathes whisky fumes into Christiansen's face, he flinches slightly from their potency. "It was visited upon Cygnus when the power blew back on him. Your corruption burned his eyes right out of his head. I've seen the empty sockets, the scars left on his face and hands. Extraordinary."

"Most extraordinary. I'll be on my way, young Lehi, but I will do so after offering one more word of warning. This mentor of yours— Cygnus." Christiansen slips his dark glasses partway down the bridge of his nose. Beneath, his eyes are dead and stony and burn with a bright phosphorescent spark in their depths. The mad, dancing glimmer is the red color of lightning in a sandstorm. "I have heard his name before, you know. I traveled between the worlds of the living and the dead for a long time, Lehi Pyburn. From what I can remember— what I learned— I'd stay away from your 'Worshipful Master.' His bill is long and detailed and will come due eventually. His name has become known to certain factions in the land of the dead. I wouldn't advise you to be near him when it all comes crashing down."

"Wouldn't you," Lehi says ruminatively. "Hmmm."

They part ways shortly thereafter. With Christiansen on

his way east (which is all the information concerning his itinerary that he is willing to share) and a stomach full of tough and over-seasoned beef, Lehi finds another bar along Main Street, a smoky little hole where he proceeds to get well and truly drunk. By the time he staggers out of its doors again, the sky is filled with the dying embers of the sunset, which has arrived in red and bloody fashion. Lehi, a little disoriented, stumbles in what he thinks must be the direction of the White House, and, before long, finds himself on the street before the Salt Lake Temple. Its capstone in place, it is almost finished, although scaffolding still bristles from the spires like black cobwebs, ready for the finishing touches to be applied. Lehi raises his eyes to the ventral crimson of the sky and the blazing, gold-plated figure of the Angel Moroni atop the Temple's tallest spire.

Except the figure he sees is not the golden angel Moroni. What he *does* see drives him to his knees in shock, dizzy, which leads to passers-by muttering "drunk" and "disgraceful." It is not the whisky that has felled him — it is the sight of the apparition that graces the top of the Temple. It is bigger

310

than Moroni ever was and bears no trumpet to announce its coming. Its wings spread wide, and its bony arms are raised to the heavens. A grinning, skeletal visage stares from above flowing robes and fleshless ribs. An apparition, a vision impossible to misinterpret or misidentify. There, crowning the bloody evening sky, the Angel of Death spreads its wings as wide as the open frontier.

Epilogue

The train snakes its way through the vast emptiness of northern Nevada. Within the train car, the floor sways gently like a flat wooden hammock, but the light is good, and Brimelow has availed himself of it to read. The gentle motion of the car and the march of text upon the page have put him into a sort of trance that is not unpleasant, and the big man relaxes against his hard seat. He can feel the bite of its unforgiving wood in his bones, and, not for the first time, Brimelow laments not so much his lost youth as the newly discovered continent of aches, pains, and humiliations that age has revealed, a rocky shore, indeed, upon which to find himself marooned.

The book that has so absorbed Brimelow is not an easy read; the cramped and spidery handwriting is a chore to decipher, and a great deal of what is discussed is well beyond Brimelow's comprehension. Regardless, he perseveres. Brimelow is a better reader now than he had been while in the employ of Leonidas Pyburn, and with practice, he's improving even more every day. Without the casual cruelties and belittlement that Leonidas had heaped upon him, Brimelow has discovered that he is actually quite bright, and his moss-green eyes diligently scan and rescan the pages before him as the train rocks.

The daylight streaming through the windows cuts rectangular swaths through the haze of dust and smoke that fills the air. In the back of the car, a group of filthy dairy-men smoke cheap cigars and mutter in low, seditious voices. Brimelow has not had occasion to engage in violence since leaving the Pyburns' employ, but it's a lifelong habit ingrained by vast experience, and his attention never truly strays from the men as he reads (they, for what it's worth, have cast more than the occasional sidelong glance in Brimelow's direction).

Perhaps it's because his attention is divided between his book and the dairy-men; perhaps he is simply losing his edge with age. Either way, when the figure slides into the seat beside him, Brimelow is taken off guard. It's a Native woman, clad in motley leathers so soft and broken-in that they make not so much as a whisper as she bends to sit. Brimelow, instincts triggered, reaches for the big knife that hangs just inside his overcoat and grimaces, bracing for trouble. Instead, as he sees her face and registers the terrible scar that mars half her welcoming grin, simple surprise relaxes his fingers as recognition washes over him.

"Mister Brimelow, was it?" asks Left Hand.

"You— you're the hunter. Left Hand. Am I correct?"

"You are," she agrees, relaxing into her seat. She shoots a look at Brimelow's hand, which still lingers inside his overcoat, and chuckles. It's a sound like broken slate shifting on a hillside. "Easy, Mister Brimelow. I mean you no harm— we're all friends here." She raises the volume of her voice to include the dairy-men in the conversation; their conversation has ceased as they quite unashamedly gawk at the unlikely pair. "We're all friends but the porter who called me an Indian bitch and told me my kind wasn't welcome in his car. Good luck for him, he *will* wake up, eventually. At least, I hope he will—I may have gotten a bit carried away." The dairy-men look at each other, shrug, and resume their muttered conversation. The air so cleared (*if only*, Brimelow thinks, eyes burning in the smoke and dust), Left Hand relaxes and turns back to Brimelow.

"What is it that has you so entranced there?" asks Left Hand, inspecting the book in Brimelow's hands. Its leather covers are so beaten and scuffed that they are practically made of suede, and the pages— slightly yellowed with age— are dog-eared. Brimelow closes the book (marking his place carefully) and considers the question for a moment before answering.

"It's a journal. To be more precise, it's the journal of Leonidas Pyburn."

"I see," says Left Hand. Her gaze is utterly unforgiving in the clarity of its question. "That seems like the sort of thing

you wouldn't be reading, had your employer's schemes suc-
ceeded. He's dead, then?" Brimelow nods. Left Hand's smile
is sardonic and an unpleasant sight. "Have you set out to
learn who you were working for all that time, then?"

"I knew who I was working for. Knew him better than
anyone on Earth. Which is how I know that there's business
he left unfinished."

"So you're running errands for a dead monster?"

Brimelow bristles at her words. "I'm running no errands,
and my employment with Mr. Pyburn ceased at the threshold of his tomb." He taps the journal with one thick fingertip.
"The young murderer can keep the house— he can keep the
gold, for all I care. The old man's real treasures were more...
esoteric. And better hidden from creditors, governments,
and murderers alike."

"Oh?" Left Hand's bright black eyes gleam. "A dead monster's treasure, then? I like that story. I have heard stories like
that since I was young enough to believe them. In time, I was
old enough not to. Now, I find that I believe again."

Brimelow carefully secrets the journal in his overcoat, in

the pocket opposite the breast where he hangs his knife, then re-shifts the coat around him. He chooses his next words with care.

"I heard," he says slowly, "about your exploits in Gold Hill. What was it, seven dead?"

"Nine," she replies easily. "But six of them weren't my doing— six dead is why they sought me out. The three I did for were the problem and the reason those first six were dead. A good deal *more* than six would have perished, if they had not found me."

"Yes, well, when I heard you described, I remembered you well. Arguably, of the fools assembled that night in the boneyard, you acquitted yourself most sensibly."

"I did what I was hired to do," she replies. "I kept the old man from having his throat torn out. When I saw the wizard spring his trap, I figured that you wašíču had it handled. Was I wrong?"

This draws a laugh from Brimelow, a hearty one that feels like it comes all the way up from the pit of his stomach. "Oh, good Jesus, yes. You were quite wrong about that.

Whatever that vile little conjurer was trying to do, it blew up in his face—quite literally. It blinded him and drove him mad. He and the young man— Lehi— they slew Leonidas two years ago."

Left Hand absorbs this in silence for a moment. "So. Your spirit still carries Leonidas like a curse. Maybe whatever's in there—" She nods in the direction of the journal, safely ensconced in his pocket. "Is worth bearing his weight. Maybe it is not."

Brimelow sighs. "And you? What's your story, then?"

"*My* story?" Left Hand laughs. Hers is no easy belly-sound; it's a jagged thing, all protesting throat and scarred soft palate. "This is no place for *my* story. Everything you wašíču build, you pretend that it was built by fathers and sons, sons and fathers. No wonder the murderousness and hunger of your people. You've no patience or subtlety for other folks' stories—even though it's the other stories that make up the biggest portion of the world, the weave and warp of it."

"I?" Brimelow sounds offended. "I've patience aplenty

for your story, Left Hand. No more sons and fathers, then."

"But still murder," Left Hand says. Her eyes are cold, their black depth taking his measure. "Still terror. I've heard tell of *your* work as well, Mister Brimelow."

"Yes," Brimelow says, and for the first time, his mossy gaze shifts to the floorboards of the train car. "I've much for which to atone—perhaps more than the Lord can forgive. Perhaps more than He *should* forgive." A moment passes in silence. The car rocks with the motion of the train, each joint and fixture creaking and rattling in the unsubtle hubbub of travel.

"My story," Left Hand says at length, "is a story of gold and monsters."

"Gold and monsters."

Brimelow rummages in a vest pocket and withdraws a half-smoked cigar, easily twice the girth of those sucked on by the dairy-men. He ignites it with a flourish of match-flame and smoke, waving his match afterward to put it out like a magician performing a trick. The dairy-men stare. "Those," says Brimelow, "are topics I know a thing or two about. Hunting monsters, though—that's a trade in which I'd eagerly apprentice, meager though the gold be."

This time, Left Hand's appraising look is almost warm. "You'd do," she admits eventually. "As an *apprentice*, that is."

Brimelow smokes in silence for a bit, mossy eyes scanning the rolling foothills outside the train's window. "Why is it," he asks Left Hand, "that we're called to such vocations? You hunt monsters, I worked for one and sought to entrap another."

Left Hand shows Brimelow her secret smile, her sharp and frozen sickle-smile.

"Haven't you guessed it yet? You and I—we're monsters, too."

Charles Bernard

About the Author

Charles R. Bernard is a writer who lives in Salt Lake City, Utah. His work has been featured in publications like Thuggish Itch and Cosmic Horror Monthly, and has appeared in anthologies like American Cult, Peaks of Madness, and Deadman Humour: 13 Fears of a Clown. He is a contributor at Madness Heart Press, where he co-hosts the podcast Wandering Monster and blogs about horror culture.

He resides next to Salt Lake City Cemetery; a sprawling necropolis whose tombs and markers stretch out over a square kilometer of grounds. Charles is lively enough company, though.

You can find him at https://www.charlesrbernard.com.

Charles Bernard

More Books from
Madness Heart Press

Broken Nails by Susan Snyder
ISBN: 979-8664122848

Treif Magic by John Baltisberger
ISBN: 978-1734893700

Extinction Peak by Lucas Mangum
ISBN: 979-8689548654

American Cult Anthology
ISBN: 978-1076432445

ALL MEN ARE TRASH by Gina Ranalli
ISBN: 978-1734893731

www.ingramcontent.com/pod-product-compliance
Lightning Source LLC
Chambersburg PA
CBHW071100250626
47159CB00002B/530

* 9 7 8 1 7 3 4 8 9 3 7 4 8 *